THE LEO M...

James Fraser was a typical Leo man,
thought Rowan—bossy! Just not to be
compared with nice René Colbert who
was so attracted to her. But when they
were all shipwrecked on a tiny island in the
tropics Rowan found herself rapidly revising her opinion of both men!

THE LEO MAN

BY

REBECCA STRATTON

MILLS & BOON LIMITED
LONDON W1

First published 1980
Australian copyright 1980
Philippine copyright 1980
This edition 1980

© Rebecca Stratton 1980

ISBN 0 263 73327 0

Set in Linotype Plantin 10 on 11 pt.

Made and printed in Great Britain by
Richard Clay (The Chaucer Press), Ltd., Bungay, Suffolk

CHAPTER ONE

FROM the very beginning Rowan had had doubts about sailing on the *Belle o' Dunoon*, and had said so to her grandmother. The first intimation she had was when Marguerite de Clare returned from a shopping expedition looking even more bright and animated than usual, and obviously bursting to tell her something. She had, she informed Rowan with breathless excitement, bumped into the son of an old friend.

'Such an attractive man,' her grandmother insisted, and Rowan made no attempt to hide her smile, for Marguerite de Clare's penchant for attractive men was no secret.

But the crunch had come a few seconds later when Marguerite blithely announced that she had, on behalf of them both, accepted an invitation to sail with the son of her old friend on his yacht. 'Cruise to the tropics lasting for several weeks, *chérie*,' she enthused, and was obviously delighted about it.

'Several weeks?' Rowan stared at her in dismay.

'Ah, but you'll enjoy it, *chérie*,' her grandmother assured her, and laid slender, soothing fingers on her arm.

'I'm not so sure,' Rowan demurred.

She was not normally so unwilling to fall in with whatever Marguerite wanted to do, but she had never been happy on the water and her grandmother knew it. Even a dinghy on a boating lake could make her feel uneasy; not because she suffered from seasickness, but simply because she did not enjoy the sensation of being on water.

'Grand'mère, you know how I feel about sailing, about being on the water in any kind of boat at all. Why did you include me?'

5

'But this isn't just any boat, child,' Marguerite pressed.
'The *Belle o' Dunoon* is a sea-going yacht, not a dinghy or
a canoe.'

'It's a boat and it sails on water,' Rowan insisted. 'You
know I'd hate it, Grand'mère; *I* know I would.'

'But it's such a wonderful opportunity.' Her grandmother's enthusiasm was undiminished, whatever her argument. 'This yacht is so beautiful, Rowan, you won't believe
how beautiful until you see it. There are no discomforts at
all, it has all the amenities of a first-class hotel.'

Rowan stared at her. Very little that her grandmother
did surprised her, but it was hard to imagine her giving
up some of her precious shopping time to look over a
boat, however luxurious. In this instance, however, that
seemed to be exactly what she had done, for her smile was
blandly satisfied and her eyes gleamed with unconcealed
pleasure.

'I've actually been aboard her,' she boasted, 'and I've
never seen anything so wonderful! Oh, Rowan, you don't
know how I always longed for a yacht. But your *grandpère*,
when he was alive, never had the time to go sailing, and
your papa doesn't like sailing; who could I share my enthusiasm with? Much as I adore sailing, in comfort mind
you, I've never fancied myself in the role of captain. No,
I prefer to be a passenger, waited on hand and foot while
we sail through tropical waters; lazy days and romantic
nights—ah!'

Marguerite could see herself in just that situation,
Rowan knew it. Her grandmother had a taste for the
exotic and revelled in the kind of situation she described.
'And you'll be waited on hand and foot on this dream ship,
will you?' Rowan asked.

'But of course! There's a steward aboard and it will
be his job to see to our comfort; of course we shall be
waited on.'

'I see.' She saw her argument as already lost, but did not

let it be known yet. 'And taking everything into account, you couldn't resist it?'

'But of course I couldn't!' said Marguerite. 'Just as I couldn't refuse the invitation on your behalf, *chérie*. How could I say that my granddaughter was afraid of being on the water?'

'You couldn't, of course; pride would forbid that!' Rowan sighed. 'Do we know any of the other people who are going?'

To Rowan, looking for loopholes, the question seemed a reasonable one, and yet for some reason her grandmother looked uneasy, and her eyes no longer met hers. 'The *Belle o' Dunoon* isn't a liner, *chérie*,' she pointed out.

'Meaning?'

Marguerite could look very matriarchal when she chose to, and she chose to now, a fact that Rowan viewed with suspicion. 'I hate crowds,' Marguerite insisted, in bland defiance of the truth. 'There will be only James himself and a friend of his who is also crewing for him, as well as three other crew members.'

Rowan stared at her in disbelief, wondering if it could possibly be all a gigantic hoax. 'That's all?' she asked.

'That's enough,' Marguerite decreed with the look that Rowan knew well enough meant that she was not going to argue the matter, but had made up her mind. 'Good heavens, I shall be there to chaperone you, child, if that's what concerns you!'

'And who's going to chaperone *you*?' Rowan demanded, not entirely in jest.

Marguerite laughed. 'Why you, of course, *chérie*!' Her bright dark eyes rolled wickedly, and she looked as far removed from the conventional idea of what a grandmother should be as it was possible to get. 'James is every bit as ruggedly charming and sexy as his father was, and I just couldn't resist going with him. What luck wasn't it, *mignonne*? Bumping into him like that and then discovering he had two spare cabins on board!'

'Incredible luck!'

Her sarcasm went unremarked, but Rowan had her own ideas on how fortuitous it was. A little probing wouldn't come amiss, she felt, to try and discover just who James Fraser might be or, more to the point perhaps, who his father was. There were any number of incidents in the past life of her sprightly and vivacious grandparent that were best left discreetly alone, but Rowan felt that if they were to go sailing off into the blue with a boat load of strangers, she would like to know something about at least one of them.

'Just who *is* James Fraser, Grand'mère?'

Marguerite's dark eyes darted sideways between lowered lashes, and her mouth had what Rowan always thought of as her pussycat look. She busied herself with something while she enlightened her too, which was quite enough to tell Rowan her guess had been correct.

'He's the youngest son of Sir Grant Fraser.'

'A Scotchman?'

'A Scot,' her grandmother corrected her. 'You should know that, being half Scots yourself, child.'

Rowan ignored the lecture and regarded her with a raised brow. 'And?'

'I knew Grant—rather well at one time. He was a very charming and attractive man, just as his son is; I've no doubt he still *is* charming and attractive, for he can't be more than—sixty-nine.'

'I see. And he was——'

'He was my lover!'

If Rowan was reticent about putting it into words, Marguerite de Clare had no such qualms. She had never admitted to the slightest regret about any of her past affairs, and to give her her due Rowan did not suspect her of having been a home-breaker; she was far too discreet for that. Just the same Rowan felt even less inclined to spend several weeks at sea with a man who was at best an embarrassing reminder of her grandmother's past.

'It was twenty-three years ago, before you were born,' Marguerite told her, taking note of her expression. 'It was when I was in Scotland for Michel's marriage to your dear mama.'

'Oh, Grand'mère, really!' Laughter inevitably mingled with reproach, for it was always so difficult to condemn Marguerite's appetite for romance. Even her son, Rowan's father, referred to her as the merry widow. 'You went to Scotland for my parents' wedding and got involved in an affair of your own—how could you?'

'Oh pooh, child!' Marguerite chided her. 'It was all very discreet—I was never less; and when I discovered that Grant was in line for a knighthood then I brought the affair to an end at once. I would do nothing to jeopardise his career, nor would I have broken up his marriage and deprived his three little sons of their father. It was an affair of only a few short weeks—a brief encounter, eh?'

Rowan made no comment, keeping her opinion to herself, but Marguerite seemed not to notice. She was always happy to remember her past lovers, although she never went beyond the bounds of discretion when she discussed them. In this instance she had said more than usual, probably because of the meeting with his son.

'I recognised James because of his likeness to his father,' she mused. 'And when he so gallantly picked up the parcel I dropped——'

'Accidentally, of course!'

'Bah! You have no romance in your heart, child!' Marguerite scolded. 'I sometimes think you've inherited nothing of the de Clares, only your dour Scottish forebears' blood!'

'I suppose you learned the meaning of dour from Sir Grant Fraser?' Rowan suggested with a mischievous smile. 'Oh, Grand'mère, you're quite incorrigible!'

'Absolutely!' Marguerite agreed readily, and rolled her eyes. She was thoroughly enjoying herself, Rowan realised, and could not find it in her heart to blame her. 'But if James is as much like his papa in other ways as he is in looks, my child, you could well be very grateful to me before the end of this cruise!'

Resigned but still fighting, Rowan shook her head. 'Grand'mère! I refuse to go on a cruise with the son of one of your ex-lovers, just so that you can relive your disreputable past through me!'

But she had come, of course, because in the ten years that Marguerite de Clare had cared for her Rowan had never yet beaten her in an argument. She had lived in France with her grandmother since she was twelve years old; ever since her Scottish mother died and she had passed into the legal custody of her father. She and Marguerite had a mutual love and admiration for one another, but even at twenty-two years old, Rowan knew that whatever her grandmother decreed would be, for Marguerite de Clare never accepted defeat.

The outcome had therefore been inevitable, and for weeks now Rowan had been making the best of what was for her an uneasy situation. She sat gazing at the endless vista of ocean and sky and wished she could enjoy herself with the same abandon that Marguerite did. She had nothing to complain of as far as the accommodation was concerned, for the *Belle o' Dunoon* was every bit as comfortable and luxurious as her grandmother had said it was. The beautiful sea-going yacht lacked nothing, but still the thought of being so far from land kept her constantly on edge.

There was the matter of their host and captain too. Marguerite loved the company of men, and had a particular liking for the virile and rather earthy type personified by James Fraser, but to Rowan he was another reason for her uneasiness, simply because he was who he was. Not that

she was shocked or embarrased by her grandmother's somewhat lurid past, but it was something new to have the attraction carried over into the second generation, and she
found their captain something of an enigma.

She had no need to turn her head to know just what the
man at the wheel looked like, for there had been oppor-
tunities enough in the past weeks to take stock of the
characteristics that made James Fraser an attractive man
in Marguerite's eyes. He was impressive, she had to admit, as he stood at the wheel looking as if he owned not
only the beautiful vessel they sailed in, but the entire ocean
as well.

Light navy slacks showed off muscular calves and lean
narrow hips, and he was taller than average too; yet in
contrast to the rest of his rangy leanness, his shoulders and
chest were broad and powerful. His complexion was so
deeply tanned that it contrasted strongly with thick tawny-
gold hair and the long pale lashes that shadowed heavy
lids. There was an air of arrogance about him too, that
put Rowan further on her guard.

Whenever she came on deck while he was taking the
watch, she had been made uneasily aware of his scrutiny,
and for that reason she usually tried to avoid being there
while he was on duty. She tried to ignore it now, but found
it alarmingly hard to do. Determined as she was, the bold
and steady regard of ice-blue eyes was eventually too disturbing, and she got up from her chair and went to lean on
the rail for a moment.

Her grandmother would almost certainly scoff at her
reaction, but then Marguerite would never understand the
feelings that gave rise to it. Her arms folded on the rail,
Rowan gazed across the glassy surface of the ocean, squint-
ing against the dancing gleams of sunlight that flashed
like living fire with every ripple, and as she stood there she
could feel that unwavering study of her going on.

'Are you bored, Rowan?'

His voice was flattened and diminished by the vast space around them, but it reached her clearly enough, and she looked across automatically. She hadn't realised how deep and audible her sigh had been as she turned to go, but he must have heard it and questioned its cause; ice-blue eyes regarded her quizzically.

A suspicion of amusement lurked in them somewhere too, and not for the first time Rowan suspected that her barely disguised wariness amused rather than annoyed him. She wished too that it was not so easy to understand her grandmother's assessment of him. He was undeniably a very virile and masculine man, and the way he looked at her sometimes was disturbingly suggestive of speculation.

'The way you look suggests you're being transported for life instead of enjoying a pleasure cruise,' James Fraser went on when she did not reply, and as she had done in the past, Rowan noted the faintly accented voice. It wasn't broad Scots, but a soft, lilting reminder of his Highland origin. 'Were you brought along under protest, Rowan?'

The way he rolled his r's made a delightful difference to her name, but she wondered why he always spoke English to her when she knew he was capable of conversing in quite passable French. It was true that his accent then had the flat harsh vowels of the Marseilles docks, but she did not understand the distinction he made. It was with the idea of letting him know she had noticed that she answered him in French; the neat tidy Parisian French that her grandmother spoke.

'I don't much like sailing,' she told him, without actually admitting that she had been given little choice in the matter of whether she came or not. 'I never have enjoyed being on the water at all.'

'Ah, I see.' His eyes scanned her flushed cheeks and evasive eyes, and if she had looked up she would have noticed the way he smiled. 'I imagine Maggie bulldozed you into it, am I right?'

He had disregarded her attempt to change to French and

continued in his own rolling brogue, which Rowan had to admit was very attractive. 'I wasn't given much choice, in fact,' she allowed. 'If I had, frankly I wouldn't be here.'

'I thought not!'

It occurred to her then that she was not exactly being polite to her host and she shook her head as a gesture of apology. 'I don't mean to sound ungrateful, Mr Fraser, but I would much rather not have come. But Grand'mère can be very persuasive, and she's enjoying herself enormously.'

'Of course, Maggie will always enjoy herself—she's that kind of woman!'

Almost without realising it, Rowan had moved up alongside the wheelhouse. The glass partitions were slid back to let what breeze there was into the confined space, and now that she stood closer to him it became even more apparent just how tall he was. It was hard to believe they had lived, eaten and slept in such close proximity for several weeks, for Rowan felt she knew him very little better now than she had at the very beginning. That brief affair of her grandmother's always stayed uneasily to the forefront of her mind, and made her more selfconscious than she would normally have been with any man.

Those light eyes were oddly disturbing too, darkened slightly at the moment by the deep blue shirt he was wearing. 'You don't approve of me calling your grannie Maggie, do you Rowan?' he asked, and something in the tone of his voice made her turn her head quickly.

She didn't like his way of calling her grandmother by that rather disreputable nickname, but Marguerite herself revelled in it, so it was hardly Rowan's place to object. In fact she knew Marguerite had laughed at the coincidence, telling him that his father had called her Maggie too. They had both laughed delightedly when he said he knew, that was why he did it, and Marguerite adored him for his impudence.

'That's up to Grand'mère,' she told him, but feared

her assumed carelessness was not altogether successful, for his mouth curved briefly into a curiously crooked smile.

'Did you know that your grannie and my father were old friends?' he asked, and Rowan glanced at him uncertainly, wondering just how enlightened he was.

'Yes, Grand'mère told me.'

'Uh-huh!' He watched her flushed face and carefully averted eyes for a moment while his guiding hands kept the yacht on course. 'And did she tell you just *how* friendly, I wonder?' A brief sight of her expression was apparently enough to confirm it, for his sudden short burst of laughter startled her, and from the corner of her eye she noticed his shaking head. 'I thought so,' he went on. 'It would account for the solemn wee po-face of you!'

'I wonder *you* find it so amusing,' Rowan challenged, and immediately wondered at herself sounding so very prim and disapproving.

'After twenty-three years I'm surprised anyone finds it anything but vaguely nostalgic,' James Fraser told her bluntly. 'All right, it was wrong, more so in those days than it would be now, but no one was hurt by it and it's long since over and done with. So why should you stand there frowning your virtuous little frown over something that happened before you were born?'

'I don't—I'm not frowning,' Rowan protested, taken aback by the suddenness and unexpectedness of the attack. 'I just——'

'I'm assuming that's the reason you've been treating me like an undesirable ever since we left Cassis,' James insisted. 'Have a heart, Rowan—I was a boy of nine when it happened, and not responsible for the behaviour of my father!'

'I didn't suggest you were,' Rowan hastened to assure him. From his point of view it must seem obvious that her attitude towards him was influenced by her knowledge of his father's indiscretion, she supposed.

'In fact,' James went on, 'it would probably be more to the point if *I* was the one to assume the air of righteous condemnation. Having met Maggie I can well believe that Father didn't have a lot of running to do; Maggie's quite a gal now, and it doesn't take a lot of imagination to see her as she must have been twenty-odd years ago.'

It was far too likely to be the truth for Rowan to be able to summon a convincing denial. Furthermore, she had the feeling that he was not so much trying to exonerate his father from blame as point out that her grandmother would have been a willing partner in seduction. Rowan was ready to admit as much, but it wasn't easy with his eyes on her, and while she was hesitating, he went on, a faint smile lurking near one corner of his mouth.

'Did it shock you, Rowan? Did you think your grannie was a virtuous old lady who'd never cast a bold eye at any man except her husband?'

Her grandmother had described James Fraser as earthy, and it seemed that at the moment he was bent on proving her right. But to Rowan his frankness on this particular subject was not only embarrassing but ill-informed, and she set out to put him right on one or two points. 'I'm fully aware of Grand'mère's penchant for attractive men,' she informed him in a light cool voice that was intended to put him firmly in his place. 'But virtuous or not, she wouldn't thank you for referring to her as an old lady, even now. As for the rest, Mr Fraser, my grandmother was as faithful a wife as any man could wish to have, while my grandfather was alive!'

He spread one hand in a gesture of supplication, but there was still a bold gleam in the ice-blue eyes that was infinitely disturbing. 'You don't have to sell Maggie to me,' he insisted, 'I like her fine.'

'Then you'll be pleased to know the admiration's mutual!'

Heaven knew what had made her say such a thing, but

quite clearly it amused him. 'Ah, well—Maggie has a way of making a man feel good,' he told her, and obviously approved of whatever it was, 'and men like her for it. She's a charmer.'

'She's an attractive woman,' Rowan agreed, and he smiled.

'But you're prettier.' He took blatant stock of her physical attributes and obviously approved of what he saw. 'Prettier than Maggie ever was, I'd say, and I'll bet those gorgeous grey eyes can give as encouraging a come-on as your grannie's ever did. Yet you've never once looked at me or said a word you haven't been obliged to.' His soft, deep laughter was discomfiting and Rowan hastily avoided his eyes. 'I know I'm not the handsomest man in the world, but that's never cramped my style yet. What I'm trying to say is that I'm not used to being treated as if I don't exist, Rowan, and it's very hard for my masculine ego.'

Rowan kept her eyes averted. There was something about the nature of his complaint that was oddly affecting, and she was more wary of him than ever for the moment. 'Mr Fraser, I——'

'That's what I mean exactly!' he interrupted swiftly, and Rowan blinked in startled surprise. 'We've been closeted together for weeks now and you're on first name terms with every other man aboard! René—*especially* René—Paul, Bill and even old Steven in the galley, they all get the chummy smile and first-name. But me? I get a po-faced acknowledgement of my existence occasionally, and a ver-r-r-y polite *Mister* Fraser!'

'I'm sorry.'

It was almost a surprise to hear herself apologising, and yet Rowan supposed she did owe him an apology if she had indeed been as unfriendly as he suggested. Undoubtedly her grandmother's story of her affair with his father had been the basis of her wary regard of him, but the man himself was oddly disturbing too. Every bit as attractive as her grandmother claimed, but something more too; and it was the unknown quantity that made her keep her distance.

'If you really are sorry, why not remedy the situation?' James Fraser suggested, and she gasped aloud when a large hand slid under her chin and raised her face so that those light, heavy-lidded eyes could look down into it. 'Try it,' he coaxed, r's rolling softly. 'It'll not hurt, I promise!'

'James.'

Rowan pronounced his name very precisely and without expression, and heard his tongue cluck in disapproval as she jerked her head to one side and evaded his hand. Her grandmother, she could guess, would have enjoyed that little interlude, but Rowan hoped she need never hear of it. If she did she would almost certainly scold her for her reaction.

'Is that the best you can do?'

It was the taunting, challenging air about him that she found most disconcerting, and Rowan automatically lifted her chin in defiance of it. 'I only know one way to pronounce James,' she told him. 'I don't know what else you expect!'

His light eyes regarded her quizzically for a moment, even though she did not look at him again. 'Have you spent much time in the U.K.?' he asked, and Rowan's immediate instinct was to object to such personal probing. But something about those watching eyes was compelling enough to overcome her natural wariness, and while she kept her eyes on the golden haze of the horizon, she gave him the briefest possible account of her rather complicated childhood.

'I was born in France, but my parents parted when I was about two and my mother took me to England with her——'

'Not to Scotland?'

Her eyes briefly questioned his knowledge, but it didn't

take much perception to realise who his informant was. 'I suppose Grand'mère told you that my mother was Scotch —Scots,' she guessed, and he nodded, a faint smile recognising her suspicion and amused by it. Rowan ran a finger along the ledge of the wheelhouse window and once more avoided looking at him. 'I don't think she could bring herself to go home and admit her marriage had failed, so she—we lived in Sussex until my mother died. Papa got custody of me and I came back to France.'

'And you've spoken French ever since.'

'I had an advantage—I started off bi-lingual as soon as I talked.'

'You've a very faint accent to your English, do you realise that?' Taken by surprise, Rowan turned swiftly and frowned at him. He was smiling, a full smile now, that gave his mouth a slightly cock-eyed look that was oddly attractive, although she hesitated to admit it, even to herself. 'A very, very slight French accent,' he went on. 'Not very pronounced, but it just turns the odd vowel into something very sexy.'

'I'm sure I haven't!'

Her denial was swift and oddly breathless, and an unfamiliar shyness made her deny it without stopping to consider that it might well be true. She had lived in France for the past ten years and it was quite likely she had acquired a slight accent when she spoke English. No one else had commented on it, but then she seldom spoke English now, and strangers were not usually so forthcoming with personal remarks as this man was.

'I assure you, you have,' he insisted, 'and I can't imagine why you're so indignant about it. It's the reason I always speak English to you; it's very—ooh la-la!'

It was time she put an end to what was proving to be a very embarrassing conversation, Rowan thought, he was much too disconcerting. Smoothing imaginary creases from her skirt, she sought to keep her voice matter-of-fact. 'I think it's time I went below,' she told him. 'It's getting rather too hot on deck.'

'Running away?' he drawled, and Rowan looked swiftly to deny it; caught a certain look in his eyes and hastily turned away again. 'Sorry!' The bright gleam in his eyes gave lie to the murmured apology, and he went on quite matter-of-factly, 'If you're going in search of René, you may as well wait up here on deck for him. He's due to relieve me on watch in less than five minutes.'

It was, in fact, exactly what she had been going to do, but the fact that the mutual attraction that she and René Colbert felt for one another had been noted and, what was more, remarked on, took her aback for a moment. Not that she really minded if James Fraser had noticed their mutual attraction, for René was more than simply a member of the crew, he was a personal friend of his, but it gave her a feeling of being under observation which she disliked, although she somehow managed to conceal it.

'Never mind,' she said, determinedly casual. 'I'll go and see him for a few minutes before he takes over.'

'Just as long as he isn't late on watch again,' James Fraser persisted, and Rowan turned back briefly, her grey eyes challenging.

'What happens if he is?' she asked. 'Do you clap him in the brig?'

She turned away hastily when he laughed, because she found it oddly disturbing somehow. 'I'd say it was more to the point if I were to clap *you* in the brig and lose the key!' he retorted. 'Since René got so—friendly with you he makes a habit of being late on watch, and friend or not, it isn't something I can keep on overlooking when I've other crew.'

Looking at him over her shoulder again, she frowned, wondering why the possibility had not occurred to her. 'I'm sorry,' she told him after a second or two, 'I didn't realise.'

'I hardly supposed you did,' he allowed with unexpected tolerance, and for a moment before she turned to go he held her uneasy gaze with unwavering steadiness. 'I didn't suspect you of trying to sabotage discipline among the crew, or I'd have said something before now, and much more to the point.'

Rowan was quite sure he would have, and she gave him a last long challenging look before she turned away, restraining the retort that sprang to mind, only with difficulty. But she was fully aware that he watched her all the way to the hatchway and until she went hurrying down the steep companionway to the saloon, a steady and, she suspected, slightly amused look.

It was hard to imagine two more different men than René Colbert and James Fraser, and yet they were the best of friends and had a seemingly genuine affection for one another. Grand'mère had discovered that their fathers had mutual business interests, but there was obviously more than that behind the long-standing friendship between them. If she had stopped to think about it, it was odd that her instant liking for René had not done something to lessen her wariness where James Fraser was concerned, but that was a subject Rowan doubted if she and René would ever see eye to eye on.

Just as Rowan anticipated, she found her grandmother serenely at ease in the cool comfort of the saloon, holding court, as Rowan was wont to tease her. Although it was furnished in the style of a British country house, with solid dark furniture and lots of gleaming brass, somehow with her vivacity and essential Frenchness, Marguerite de Clare managed to endow it with the atmosphere of a turn-of-the-century Paris *salon*, subduing the down-to-earth smells of leather and brass polish with a heady French perfume, and a delightful air of slightly risqué sophistication.

She was not a pretty woman, and in her middle years her once svelte figure was becoming frankly plump, but she had the gift of being able to make men forget that she was approaching sixty and going grey. She spoke quite good English when it was required of her, but preferred to converse in her own tongue, using slim, beringed hands to emphasise some point she wished to make.

Seen in close proximity to her granddaughter it was easy to give credence to James Fraser's opinion that Rowan had the edge where looks were concerned. There was a softness in Rowan's features that had no place in Marguerite's vivid personality, and Rowan was not so tall either, with a small but very feminine shape that expensive dressing made the most of.

Rowan's hair too, was not the sable black of the older woman's, but a rich dark brown, inherited from her father, Marguerite's son, and her eyes were large and grey with heavy dark lashes, a legacy from her Scottish mother. Her complexion too was cream and pink as her mother's had been, and her mouth had the same soft fullness that could look irresistibly appealing on occasion.

Rowan was just as accustomed as her grandmother was to commanding masculine attention, and the kind of expression that showed in the eyes of René Colbert the moment he noticed her coming into the saloon. She smiled when he got to his feet, relaxing a little, and the wariness in her grey eyes changing to warmth.

René was handsome and very French and he made no secret of his feeling for Rowan, although Rowan herself sometimes suspected that it was not nearly as fervent as his manner suggested, and was not meant to be taken too seriously. Not much more than average height, he was slimly built, with dark hair that he wore fairly long and which curled slightly in the best romantic tradition, just above his ears.

His eyes were blue, a deep dark blue, not the icy paleness of his friend and captain's, and they had a certain look of innocence that did not go with the reputation that her grandmother attributed to him. He was perhaps twenty-five or six years old and did not look at all the type of man Rowan envisaged as part of a yacht's crew, for he had a certain air of delicacy about him that suggested a life of ease and comfort rather than rugged seamanship.

Marguerite de Clare had been enjoying herself, with René seated beside her and Paul Ordin, the steward, hovering in appreciative attendance, but she welcomed her granddaughter's appearance with genuine affection, holding out her hands to her as she came to join her. René placed a chair for her and managed somehow to brush his slim fingers across Rowan's neck in a shiver-inducing caress.

'Ah, Rowan, you've come to join us!' Kindly but shrewd dark eyes took note of the flush on Rowan's cheeks and the lingering darkness in her grey eyes. 'You looked so cross when you came in—whatever's the matter, child? If you frown so much you'll have wrinkles before you're thirty!' She smoothed light fingers down the space between Rowan's brows, leaning towards her and bringing with her a cloud of exotic perfume. 'What is it, *ma chère*?'

'Nothing, Grand'mère.'

'Nothing, nonsense!' Marguerite insisted. 'I thought, as you were on deck, you might have been keeping James company; instead you looked more as if you've been—made to swab the decks, or whatever it is they do to shanghaied sailors.'

Her grandmother could be relied upon to draw attention to the very thing one hoped would pass unremarked, Rowan thought ruefully, and noted from the corner of her eye that René did not like that allusion to her keeping James Fraser company. 'I'm glad you admit I *was* shanghaied,' Rowan murmured, and did not intend anyone but her grandmother to hear what she said.

'Nonsense!' Marguerite denied, and was not at all averse to an audience. 'This is the chance of a lifetime, child, and you should be grateful to me for getting you invited.'

'I didn't realise you didn't want to come.' René's anxious voice brought her head round towards him, and she noticed how he glanced down anxiously at the watch on her wrist as he spoke. 'Why, Rowan?'

The almost unconscious gesture of looking at his watch, reminded Rowan of the very recent warning she had been given in connection with René's time-keeping. Obviously James Fraser had expected her to do something to remedy René's default, and she supposed she should do something, although just what she couldn't think at the moment.

'You do look rather unhappy,' René told her as he sat in the chair next to hers and took her hand in his, looking at her in that curiously anxious way he had. 'I'm sorry you're not enjoying the trip, Rowan, I wish there was something I could do to make you less unhappy.'

Rowan found herself comparing his pronunciation of her name with the soft, rolling-r'd version of James Fraser, and she shook her head suddenly; impatient with herself rather than René. 'I'm not unhappy in the least,' she told him. 'Why should I be?'

'Heaven knows,' her grandmother interposed, 'but you looked very out of temper when you came in, child. Had you been unkind to poor James again? Sometimes I wonder he doesn't tell you what he thinks of you acting as if you can't wait for this cruise to end.'

'He just did!' Rowan informed her rashly, and once more caught the slightly anxious look René gave her. 'At least he said he didn't understand why I always looked as if I was being transported for life instead of taking a pleasure cruise—and I explained that I didn't like boats or water.'

'And you quarrelled?'

'No, we didn't! He asked, I explained. I was horribly hot and sticky sitting up there on deck, so I came down here in the cool, and that's all! The heat is absolutely unbearable!'

Marguerite looked so cool herself that it was difficult to imagine her ever looking hot and flustered, whatever the

circumstances, and her smile suggested that she saw
Rowan's complaint about the heat as yet another mark
against their host. 'Of course it's hot,' she told her, 'we
are in the tropics, child. It's fortunate that this lovely boat
of James' is air-conditioned and we don't have to suffer
because of it; although he must be far less comfortable
up there in that glass box, poor darling.'

Rowan, whose recent interview with him had aroused no
such sympathy, shook her head. 'He looked quite happy
when I saw him,' she said. 'He had the panels pushed
open and he showed no sign of wilting. I must say I
envied him when I was drooping with the heat.'

René was again reminded of his watch, Rowan noticed,
for he glanced several times in succession at his wrist-watch,
but remained where he was for the moment. He was evidently unwilling to leave now that she had joined them,
and it was a situation that Rowan viewed with mixed feelings.

'I'm due to relieve him on watch,' he said without making
a move. 'Only I shan't be as comfortable as James is. He's
used to the tropics; he's spent years in climates like this.'

'So he told me,' said Marguerite, and obviously saw it
as another point in James Fraser's favour, although she
received little encouragement from her granddaughter's
apparently disinterested face. 'He's an adventurer in the
old tradition, eh?' She ticked off the countries their host
had visited, on her fingers, and never once took her eyes
off Rowan's face; obviously she was hoping to impress her.
'Africa, Sumatra, Malaysia, South America—such a man!'

'A rover,' René remarked, seemingly with a touch of
envy for his friend's travelling record. 'I would give much
to have lived as James has; to have travelled as he has,
and done so many things.'

'And learned to cuss in so many different languages!'
added Marguerite, and laughed at René's faintly shocked
expression, stroking his cheek with light fingers. 'But I
remember he was a very adventurous little boy too,' she

went on. 'He was always getting into scrapes and being soundly beaten for it, but it didn't make a scrap of difference. He was more of a handful than his two older brothers put together.'

Her knowledge of the subject obviously intrigued René, and he prepared to listen to more if the signs were correct, so that Rowan became slightly apprehensive on two counts. Partly because she knew it must be well past the time when he should have relieved James at the wheel, and partly because she hoped her grandmother wasn't going to be too indiscreet about the source of her information.

'You knew James when he was a boy?' René asked, and Rowan recognised a curious cat-like quality in Marguerite's smile.

'I saw him only twice,' she told him, 'but I was told about him by his parents. There is a rather tenuous relationship to our family through marriage.'

If René was surprised by the revelation, Rowan was stunned by it and she stared at her grandmother in disbelief. 'I didn't know anything about that, Grand'mère,' she said, and made her doubt quite plain by the tone of her voice.

'Didn't you, child?' Marguerite eyed her, patently delighted with the effect of her bombshell. 'I can't think why not, it's not a secret.'

'Are you sure?'

Marguerite pursed her lip in dislike at being doubted, and raised her fine brows. 'Certainly I'm sure,' she insisted. 'Now let me see; James' Uncle George is married to your grandfather's sister. It's a tenuous relationship, as I said, but a factual one for all that, and it's the reason the Frasers were at your parents' wedding. James was only nine years old then, of course, and known as Jamie.'

'He's still called Jamie by his family,' René told her with

a faintly malicious grin, 'although he doesn't like it very much.'

Rowan made a note of the fact, though with what intent she had no idea as yet, it was just that it struck her as a very tiny chink in the formidable armour of James Fraser's confident superiority. Marguerite de Clare, needless to say, looked sympathetic. 'Of course he doesn't like it,' she said. 'Jamie is a little boy's name, and James is such a forceful man. Did you know,' she went on, addressing herself to Rowan, 'that he's Leo? It's inevitable, of course, with such a personality.'

One of her grandmother's passions was the study of astrology, and over the years Rowan had become quite familiar with most of the jargon connected with it. 'I'm not surprised,' she remarked, restraining an almost irresistible desire to wink an eye at René. 'Leos are supposed to be bossy, aren't they?'

René, she thought, looked slightly surprised, but her grandmother was plainly reproachful and frowned at her. 'James is a very strong character,' she insisted, 'and being in charge of a trip like this, a man needs to be strong. Someone, my child, has to be the boss in a situation like this or where would we all be?'

'You're right, of course, *madame*,' René hastened to assure her, and the glance he gave Rowan suggested that he still did not understand her attitude towards his friend. 'James is a born leader, and I'd trust him with my life.'

'A Leo man,' Marguerite agreed with unshakable confidence. 'I too would trust him with my life.'

Seeing them both so confidently in agreement, Rowan realised her support was neither needed nor expected. But she too, she thought, would probably trust her life to James Fraser, although she hoped the need to prove it would never arise.

CHAPTER TWO

IT seemed to Rowan that it was even hotter than yesterday as she lay full length in a canvas deck-chair set up under a striped awning, and she felt oddly restless without knowing quite why. It could have to do with the climate, she supposed, for the air was heavy and oppressive and seemed to enclose them in a sphere of heat, even though there was actually more wind than there had been for several days. But it was a heavy, sultry wind that did nothing to relieve the humidity at all.

Below deck the cabins and the saloon were air-conditioned, but even there Rowan had felt that sense of expectancy that prickled her scalp, and sent her up on deck in search of relief. It was her first visit to the tropics and she had vowed to herself that she would not readily repeat the experience, however fortuitous the circumstances.

By just turning her head she could catch a glimpse of René taking his turn at the wheel, and she had even more sympathy for him in the prickling, overwhelming heat. Only an unshakable lethargy kept her from going over and keeping him company for a little while, and she felt rather mean for not going. Several times she was aware of the dark blank lenses that shielded his eyes being turned in her direction, but it was unbearably hot where he was and at least under the deck awning there was a little relief from it.

Another chair was set out beside hers, but was so far unoccupied and likely to remain so, for her grandmother very seldom sat out on deck. Sitting in the sun ruined the complexion, she had warned Rowan, a warning that went unheeded because Rowan enjoyed the outdoors in a way that Marguerite never had. It had something to do with her Scottish mother, she supposed, as she lay back and gazed narrow-eyed at the relentless glitter of the sea.

She was once again trying to arouse sufficient energy to go and have a word with René when a shadow fell across her briefly, and she turned and looked up, thinking that perhaps her grandmother had decided to join her on deck after all. Instead, when she looked round she found James Fraser in the act of lowering his long length into the chair next to hers. His appearance was so unexpected that for a moment she stared at him, her pulse reacting with agitated urgency at the sight of him.

'You don't mind, do you?' Something in his voice and the suggestion of amusement in the look he gave her brought colour to her cheeks, and she shook her head.

'Why on earth should I mind?' she countered, then reminded herself that he was owner as well as captain of the yacht they were travelling in. 'It's your boat anyway, I could hardly object to anything you choose to do aboard her.'

'True!' He sent René a brief and casual salute before settling himself down. Clasping his hands behind his head, he relaxed his long muscular body to the curve of the chair, his legs extending some distance beyond the end of the footrest. Unlike René he did not wear sunglasses and the heavy lids with their fringe of pale lashes were half-closed over light blue eyes. There was something very physical, almost sensual, in the way he relaxed and gazed at her for a moment before going on. 'If the *Belle* wasn't mine *would* you object to me joining you?' he asked, and Rowan had no doubt at all that she was being challenged to deny it.

It was very seldom that any man made her feel as James Fraser did, and she coped hastily with the customary wariness she always felt whenever he came near her. Keeping her gaze forward and narrowed against the glare of the sun on the water, she once more shook her head. 'That's too provoking to deserve an answer,' she told him.

'Is it?'

Something in his voice trickled like icewater through her veins, and she stirred uneasily in her chair. She had accused him of being provoking and she believed it, but she could not imagine why he bothered to act as he did when it would have been so much easier to simply be formally polite and leave it at that.

'I think you know it is,' she insisted, trying to keep cool and unruffled if it was possible. 'And if you're looking for someone to—fight with, Mr Fraser, please don't pick on me, I'm feeling much too limp to rise to anyone's bait at the moment!'

'Fight with?' From his expression it could have been thought that nothing was further from his mind, but Rowan felt she knew better. 'I never fight with females, Rowan, and particularly not with pretty ones, however determinedly unfriendly they are. Incidentally, did you forget we dispensed with that Mr Fraser nonsense yesterday? Or am I still to be given the cold shoulder?'

She had forgotten, in fact, and she supposed it would be unreasonable of her not to admit it, so she ventured an apology without turning her head while she did so. 'I'm sorry, I'd forgotten about yesterday—James.'

'That's better!'

The somewhat paternal air of approval brought an immediate response, and Rowan remembered something that had been said yesterday. Something her grandmother had mentioned and René had confirmed; something that in the present situation seemed irresistible.

'Or maybe you prefer Jamie?' she suggested, and pretended not to hear the oath he muttered under his breath.

'Now where did you get hold of that?' he demanded, though it was as much amusement as annoyance that made his eyes gleam the way they did, Rowan felt sure. 'Who was it, Rowan?'

'Grand'mère.'

He raised his eyes to heaven and shook his head, exaggerating his normally faint accent. 'Och, Maggie, Maggie, how could ye!'

'And René confirmed it,' Rowan went on, not without satisfaction. 'He says your family still call you Jamie.'

'And so they do,' James confirmed ruefully, 'but family habits are hard to break. However, I'll not have it put in your hands as a weapon to use against me; you'll call me James, *not* Jamie, or I'll have something to say about it!'

'Don't you like it?' she challenged, knowing the answer well enough, and he eyed her narrowly.

'I've outgrown it,' he said. 'And I'm not the type of man anyone calls Jamie!'

'Grand'mère said that too.'

'Aye, well, I'm glad she went that far towards repairing the harm she might have done by passing on the information!' He half-turned his head and Rowan felt his gaze on her, steady and oddly disturbing. 'Did you agree with her?' he asked, and just briefly she glanced at him. 'Or do I strike you as a Jamie rather than a James?' he insisted.

Determinedly casual, she shrugged her shoulders. 'I hadn't thought about it,' she said untruthfully, and tightened her hands into fists at her side when she heard him laugh shortly.

'You're a funny girl, Rowan,' he remarked lazily, 'and I have to admit I don't begin to understand you. I find it hard to believe you react to me as you do simply because of that nonsense between my pa and your grannie all those years ago, but what other reason is there?'

Such incredible conceit, Rowan thought, must surely deserve a knock, but at the moment she could not think of a suitably crushing reply. 'I can hardly blame you for what happened then,' she told him, and he made a murmur suggestive of satisfaction.

'Then smile, damn you!'

But Rowan merely flicked a brief glance in his direction before resuming her study of the seemingly endless ocean. She guessed that if her grandmother had not made such a point of saying that he was every bit as charming and sexy as his father had been, and hinted that before the cruise ended Rowan might have reason to thank her for introducing her to him, she would have started off quite differently with James Fraser. She would almost certainly have taken him at face value and quite probably succumbed willingly to his undoubted attraction; enjoying his constant proximity instead of feeling suspicious and uneasy with him.

She caught her breath audibly when a large hand grasped her chin and turned her face towards him, bringing her under the close scrutiny of light, discerning eyes. 'Come on, Rowan, I'll not eat you, I promise!' His voice rolled the r in her name softly and seductively and she found it almost irresistible to look up at him while he studied her with a curiously disturbing intensity. 'Was it something else your grannie said that makes you shy from me?' he asked, and came too close to the truth for comfort.

'No—no, of course not.'

There was a depth in his voice that told her he was still smiling. 'I've no designs on your virtue, if that's what's worrying you,' he assured her. 'Not without your full consent anyway!'

'That's *very* unlikely!'

Rowan jerked her head aside and coloured furiously because the way he laughed mocked her reaction more than any words could have done. She started to get up from her chair, but was clumsy in her haste and caught her right foot on the footrest. So that instead of making a dignified withdrawal she went sprawling across James, stretched out in the other chair.

There was nothing she could do but land on his lap, and the moment she did his arms folded around her, hugging her close to the broad warmth of his chest. It was automatic to put a hand on the expanse of white shirt, but the very responsive flesh beneath it beat and throbbed with such life that she drew back at once and pressed the backs of her fingers to her mouth.

Close to, there was nothing icy about the light blue eyes between thick fringing lashes, pale as corn-silk on heavy lids. There was an earthy and very masculine touch in the body that supported her, and Rowan did her best to steady the sudden violence of her pulse. Her grandmother had said he was a very virile and sexy man and at the moment Rowan was in no position to deny it, but she had no intention of reacting in the way Marguerite would probably expect her to.

'I'm sorry,' she murmured, and struggled to sit upright rather than remain sprawled across his chest. 'I—I must have caught my foot.'

But her efforts to free herself were ignored and the enfolding arms held her as closely as ever, his voice breathing warmly against her cheek. 'Did you hurt yourself?'

'No. No, I'm perfectly all right, thank you.' Again she endeavoured to sit up and free herself for one large hand curved far too intimately under her breast. 'Please let me get up, Mr Fraser.' Long fingers pressed hard in a reprimand and she caught her breath. 'James,' she amended hastily, 'please let me get up!'

The blue eyes below their heavy lids mocked her anxiety, and his voice was pitched low as he cast a swift glance in René's direction. 'Are you worried about René thinking the worst?' he challenged, and Rowan shook her head.

'He wouldn't, he knows I don't like——'

She bit off the word quickly, but it seemed he was more amused than insulted still, though she couldn't see his eyes.

'That you don't like me?' he suggested. 'Or that you try very *hard* not to like me? You've a very wrong view of *mon ami* René if you think he won't think the worst about you being on my lap,' he told her. 'He doesn't trust me any further than he can throw me, within kissing distance of a pretty woman, especially when he hasn't got a really strong claim to her yet.' His strong teeth gleamed for a moment in an alarmingly ferocious smile. 'He hasn't, has he, Rowan? Only we never cheat one another.'

'It's none of your business!' Rowan declared, her colour high. 'And please let me go!'

Rowan struggled against the encircling arm and got to her feet somehow, catching her breath when assistance came from two big hands clasped tightly around her waist. Ruffled and conscious of her loss of dignity, Rowan stood for a moment brushing imaginary creases from her skirt. Her legs were incredibly unsteady and her hands too were shaking as she brushed vigorously. René was bound to have seen what happened and she could not imagine what he must be thinking.

She chanced a brief glance at James Fraser and noticed how relaxed he appeared. His mouth suggested a hint of a smile and he was watching her with that same quizzical, heavy-lidded look while he stretched out his long length in the chair. Like some enormous, sleek and lazy cat, she told herself maliciously, and hastily avoided his steady gaze.

'You've probably enjoyed seeing me make a fool of myself,' she accused, and he cut her short with a curt dismissive wave of his hand.

'Oh, for God's sake don't make such a major issue of it, girl!' he told her. 'I'm quite sure mine isn't the first lap you've sat on, and I've cradled more than one pretty little——'

'No doubt,' said Rowan, cutting him short hastily. 'But

it was accidental, and I'd hate you to get the idea that I did it on purpose.'

'Oh, perish the thought!' James declared. 'I know you better than to suspect that; although mebbe I should have kissed you soundly when you were down here, and smoothed out that prissy little mouth for you!'

When he reached out a hand it appeared he might be about to remedy the omission, and Rowan skipped hastily out of reach, furious with him because he laughed. Turning quickly, she made for the companionway and paid no heed to René's rather plaintive *au revoir*. James Fraser was not only arrogant and over-confident, but alarmingly affecting too, and she vowed she would stay out of his way more determinedly than ever from then on.

It was no use hoping that René hadn't noticed the incident with James earlier in the day, and obviously he was curious to know exactly what had happened. It was while she and René were on deck that same evening that Rowan tried to explain, and found her listener much more suspicious than she anticipated.

They were leaning on the rail and looking at an ocean that was ruffled into white horses before a surprisingly brisk wind. A waning moon made intermittent appearances among banks of rolling cumulus cloud and Rowan eyed its increasing volume rather anxiously. René's hand on her arm brought her back to the matter in hand, and she shrugged, treating it as carelessly as James had intimated she should.

'It was nothing at all, in fact,' she said.

'You were sitting on James' lap,' René pointed out in a rather primly pedantic tone. 'That's unusual enough to cause comment, in view of your professed opinion of him.'

'I *fell* on to James' lap,' Rowan corrected him, and inwardly condemned him for wanting it spelled out, as if she was being called upon to account for some misdemeanour. 'It was simply an accident and really not important at all,

René, nothing to make a fuss about.' She hoped she had given him the opening that allowed him to dismiss it, but there was a curiously unfamiliar look about René's mouth that somehow dismayed her. 'I got up from my chair and somehow or other managed to catch my foot in the foot-rest. The next thing I knew I lost my balance and went sprawling across his lap; I felt an absolute idiot, and *he* laughed, of course!'

René's boyishly round eyes had narrowed slightly and they looked so dark in the moonlight it was easier to believe they were black rather than blue. 'He didn't—trip you? I mean, he didn't pull you off balance or anything like that?' he added quickly when he saw her about to deny it, and Rowan looked at him for a moment in disbelief.

'Are you serious?' she asked, and could guess that he flushed under her demanding gaze.

'Quite serious,' he said, and went on hurriedly, as if he needed to explain his meaning, 'I know him better than you do, Rowan, and I know his reputation with women. I like him a lot, but his reputation——'

'One you share, according to Grand'mère,' Rowan suggested, trying to be fair, and René admitted it with a light shrug, though he would obviously rather not have done.

'Maybe,' he allowed. 'But I must be more certain that he knows you're my girl, then he'll watch his step.'

It was the first time René had laid claim to her so definitely, and Rowan recalled that James Fraser had questioned the strength of René's claim. She was not of a mind to become too serious with anyone at the moment, but she supposed that if she became serious about anyone during this trip it would be with René; certainly it wouldn't be James.

A hot sultry wind stirred the hair on her neck and Rowan half closed her eyes in appreciation, not looking at René, but at the moon dancing among the gathering clouds. And she chose her words with care. 'I don't think of myself as anyone's girl,' she told him after a moment or two. 'I really don't want to be—committed, René, not at the moment.'

'Nothing to do with James?'

He was bound to ask that, of course, in the circumstances, and she shook her head without hesitation. 'Certainly nothing to do with James Fraser,' she affirmed, and he turned and looked at her, curiously, she thought. 'It's just that I prefer to remain uninvolved at the moment, René, that's all.'

Maybe he was convinced, maybe he wasn't, but he had apparently mentioned the subject to her grandmother because it seemed he knew exactly how Marguerite felt. 'Madame de Clare thinks it's high time you got married,' he told her. 'She was married at eighteen herself, and so was your father, I understand. Madame thinks you're very tardy, still being single at twenty-two.'

Thankful for the semi-darkness, Rowan laughed and shook her head. 'I can't help how Grand'mère feels,' she told him. 'I don't intend marrying anyone until I'm sure he's the right man, and I mean *quite* sure!'

René stroked a light forefinger over the warmth of her cheek, down her slender neck to her shoulder, and followed the natural curve to the soft swell of her breast where the neckline of her blouse dipped into a vee. 'And you're sure I'm not the man, Rowan?' he asked, his finger-tip lingering seductively for a second or two.

'I'm not sure of anything at the moment,' Rowan confessed, and noticed how huskily breathless her voice was. René Colbert was all too persuasive, and she had seldom felt more vulnerable to persuasion.

Leaning forward, he pressed his lips to the soft skin of her neck. 'But you'll keep me in mind when you decide,' he urged. 'Promise me you'll do that, Rowan.'

'I'll keep you in mind,' she promised, but even as she said it she wondered if she wasn't being a little too rash.

'I love you, remember that too,' he pressed, and she nodded, omitting a verbal promise that time. René took her hand raised it to his lips, kissing her finger-tips one by one. 'I'll tell James you're off limits!' He leaned and kissed her mouth. 'I want to marry you, Rowan.'

He whispered the words so softly that even Rowan, who was so close, barely heard the words. Even so her heart began to thud violently and a pulse fluttered urgently at the base of her throat, as she looked out at the moon darting flirtatiously between one cloud and another. Maybe her grandmother had had matchmaking in mind when she accepted the invitation to come cruising in the tropics, but if she did Rowan felt sure she would have had James Fraser in mind, not René. Rowan herself was not inclined towards either as a husband at the moment, and she eased her hand free as gently as possible as she replied.

'I'm very flattered, René,' she told him in a slightly regretful voice, for it wasn't every day that a girl got a proposal from someone as desirably eligible as René Colbert. 'But I'm in no hurry to get married, whatever Grand'-mère's feelings are.'

He shrugged his shoulders resignedly and pursed his lips. 'But you do not dislike me enough to dismiss me out of hand?'

'Oh no, of course I don't!'

It was instinct that made her move aside slightly when she noticed someone coming from below deck, and she heard René's tongue cluck in annoyance. 'James going on watch,' he remarked.

Rowan consulted her wrist-watch. 'It's getting late, I think I'll turn in,' she said. 'Goodnight, René.'

'Goodnight, my darling.' He kissed her lips, and Rowan didn't understand why she felt so relieved that James had appeared when he did.

Rowan had been in a deep sleep and consciousness came

only slowly at first. She had been plagued by a curious sense of foreboding all day and something told her that this was the culmination. She hadn't really expected to sleep much, especially after René's unexpected pronouncement after dinner, but contrary to expectation she had gone off almost at once. She had dreamed too, a rather disconcerting dream in which René and James Fraser had fought one another for her favours.

In the dream James had appeared with an enormous golden leonine head, and she had felt a strange mingling of fear and excitement at his approach; a reaction that made her pulse race wildly. It was the hard, pounding beat of her heart that dragged her from sleep and into awareness, and she lay for a moment or two, trying to identify the loud roaring noise that seemed to fill the cabin.

The whole world around her seemed to be pitching and rolling and she was almost flung on to the floor of the cabin. Sleep retreated further still before the cold chill of physical fear. She sat up, alert to the hissing rattle of rain on the port, lashed by the fury of a hurricane force wind that roared across the deck and through the rigging. She was trembling like a leaf and unable to move for a moment. The possibility of a storm at sea, she realised suddenly, was something that had always been at the back of her mind from the time the trip was first mooted; but as she sat there in her bunk listening to its rising fury, a flutter of panic raced chillingly along her spine.

It took a real effort of determination to get out of bed, but if they were to be tumbled and tossed all over the ocean, she would rather be dressed and have her wits about her. Her legs trembling, she fought off the dregs of sleep and grabbed the edge of the bunk when she was almost flung off her feet by a sudden lurch that sent the things on the dressing table sliding and tinkling together before they dropped on to the carpeted floor.

She had switched on the light automatically when she

woke, but it flickered and died suddenly, plunging her into pitch blackness, before coming briefly to life again. It seemed more imperative than ever to get dressed, and she reached blindly for the clothes she had taken off earlier, dragging on a cotton skirt and shirt over the minimum of underclothes. It was necessary to grab repeatedly for the edge of the bunk to keep herself on her feet, and she had scarcely finished fumbling with the buttons on her shirt when she was pitched forward suddenly on to the floor. Over and over she rolled, tipped helplessly in the direction of the door, where she lay for a moment with all the breath knocked out of her, before struggling to her feet.

Above the violence of the storm she heard a man's voice suddenly, then the darkness seemed to explode with a roar that shook the yacht from stem to stern like a child with a toy boat. The howl of the wind seemed to follow immediately like a scream of terror, and standing there in the absolute darkness Rowan was stiff with fear as the yacht rolled and pitched, floundering helplessly.

'Rowan, Rowan!' The voice that called her repeatedly was muffled by the storm and unrecognisable, and seconds later a hand pounded on her door. A body surged through the opening, a dark unidentifiable shape that somehow found her in the darkness and grabbed her tightly. 'Thank God!' She recognised René's voice and allowed herself to be hauled almost bodily after him, with no idea of where he was taking her. 'Hurry, Rowan, for God's sake hurry! James is trying to hold her, but if the steering goes——'

Outside in the narrow passageway it was even blacker, and Rowan groped blindly for a hold on the shiny wooden bulkhead, trusting René to lead her to safety. It was instinct alone that made her realise they were passing her grandmother's cabin, and she hung back against the hand that would literally have dragged her on.

'Grand'mère!' She shrieked to make herself heard. 'Grand'mère!'

René jerked roughly at her captive hand, forcing her past the blacker void of an open door that was only faintly discernible in the surrounding blackness. 'She's in the boat with the others!' he shouted, harsh in his anxiety. 'Come on, Rowan! Oh, my God, if only I'd known my way around in the dark I wouldn't have mistaken your cabin! We've been holed and now the steering's gone; just now, I felt —Oh, God!'

Stumbling up the companionway which was under their feet before she expected it, Rowan clung to the flimsy rail and gasped at the first violent assault of the wind on deck. It was dark, but not quite the same stygian blackness as below deck, and she could just make out the gleaming glass panels of the wheelhouse and beyond it some shadowy shape by the rail that was almost swept overboard while she watched.

Scarcely able to stay on her feet, she clung to René with one hand while she tried to find a firmer grip on something more solid with the other. 'Where's James?' She screeched in competition with the wind as the yacht wallowed heavily with the water that poured in through her side.

Rowan thought she knew where James was, and the danger he was in appalled her. But René was concerned with only one thing and he dragged her relentlessly to the side of the yacht, raising an arm and ducking instinctively when a huge sheet of water broke over them; their feet slipping and sliding in the chill, sucking backwash.

'Oh, my God!' She heard René's moan of despair while she stood panting and trying to recover her breath, seeing him staring down in to the blackness. 'They've gone! The boat's gone! They've cut it loose and gone without us!'

'Grand'mère!' Her cry was borne on the wind and expressed her sense of being abandoned, even though in dif-

ferent circumstances she would have realised that the little
dinghy stood no chance at all while it was in the vicinity of
the yacht. Better to save a few than none at all.

'They took the only boat!' René wailed his anguish at
the top of his voice, and flung an arm across his eyes to
clear his vision. 'If James——'

'He wouldn't!' Rowan recalled the shadowy figure she
had seen very nearly washed overboard, and her heart
lurched sickeningly. 'He's over near the rail, René, I saw
him!'

Helpless and frustrated, René yelled his complaints to
the wind. '*He* should have come for you!' He sounded
close to tears and he clung to her hand tightly. 'He knows
his way around down there in the dark, but he sent me because—— Oh, damn him, he can't *do* anything more, she's
done for! The radio's out, the steering's gone—she's done
for!'

Not quite central, the tall mast of the yacht soared upward into the storm, lit like a sword of Damocles every time
a flash of lightning streaked along its wet shiny length,
and the tattered sails flapped like broken wings, while the
boom swung crazily. The beautiful *Belle o' Dunoon* was
dying before their eyes, and whatever else she had to
trouble her, Rowan found it heartbreaking. She knew, too,
that James Fraser was not going to desert her until he had
to.

'*Look out!*'

It was instinctive to turn in the direction of James' voice
shouting at them from the darkness. But whereas Rowan
turned, René ducked and the swinging boom passed over
him and struck her a glancing blow to the side of her head.
It was the last thing Rowan was conscious of for several
minutes, and when she eventually opened her eyes again
she cried out in fear of the vast swell of water around her.

The wind whipped it to foam-topped boulders that
hissed and lashed at her face until she closed her eyes again

to stop the stinging hurt of it. 'Ah!' The single syllable was almost drowned in the noise of the sea, and it was a moment or two before she realised she was being supported by another, much longer, body that kicked out rhythmically and somehow managed to propel them along.

An arm curved around her, just below her breast, and the other swept up and over in a slow laborious arc, again and again, but very obviously tiring. 'O.K.?' The voice spat words above her head, and she supposed she nodded, for the enfolding arm was withdrawn. 'Swim!' the voice admonished harshly, and she was bundled unceremoniously over on to her stomach then given a propelling shove forward by a large hand in her back. 'Swim for your life, girl, come on! Swim, damn your hide, move your arms and get going, come on! I'm not going to lose you now!'

The urgent cursing finally had the desired effect, and Rowan began to swim automatically, arm over arm, with James Fraser beside her, righting his own position and finding new strength now that he had only himself to propel through the water. She would never have dared attempt it on her own, but there was something incredibly reassuring about the long lean shape in the water beside her, and just for a second when she turned her head, Rowan would have sworn he gave her a wide, encouraging grin.

'Keep going—come on!'

The oddly distant voice snatched her back to realisation and she renewed her efforts. She had never before tried swimming in such conditions, and her whole body felt battered and buffeted, her arms seemingly weighted with lead as she ploughed through the huge swell. If it had not been for that lean, vigorous form and sweeping arms alongside she knew she would have given up, but while he kept as close as conditions allowed and yelled curses and exhortations at her above the roar of the sea she kept going.

'James!'

The cry came only faintly from the other side of him,

and for the first time Rowan gave a thought to the fact that René was still with them. She saw James' great leonine head lift from the water briefly and fling the hair back from his face, then he veered off away from her. His going brought Rowan a sense of panic, but as she opened her mouth to cry out her feet touched bottom and she caught her breath in a sob of unbelievable relief.

Just off to her left James made the same discovery and she saw him rise waist-high among the rolling breakers that hissed and roared their way up on to the shore in great spumes of white spray. Her legs felt too weak to stand, and the running tide beneath her feet almost swept her back again, only a hand in the small of her back, thrusting hard, enabled her to make it through the breakers.

The moment he was sure of her safety, he turned back for René, hauling him bodily from the water. There was a curious luminosity ashore that made it just possible to distinguish shapes, and from her own position face down on the wet sand, Rowan gazed at the two figures close by. As if from sheer perversity, the storm seemed to be abating too, and it was possible to identify other sounds than the deafening roar of the wind.

René too lay full length and face down, his head turned sideways to present a horribly lifeless-seeming profile with closed eyes and a gaping mouth. James knelt beside him, his strength spent for the moment, bent double and dragging air into his lungs in great gasping gulps that even the thudding crash of the breakers could not drown out. His head was bowed and from the thick mass of hair over his forehead water dripped on to the sand between his knees. It was easy to guess that his eyes were closed, but the moment he realised she had crawled across to him he lifted his head and Rowan noticed how the water clung in darkening drops to his pale lashes.

'Are you O.K., Rowan?'

His voice had a rasping harshness and the words came

out jerkily, as if he found it difficult to speak at all. Rowan
nodded, looking down at René, limp and immobile, just as
James had laid him there, and she gnawed anxiously at her
lower lip. 'René?' Her own voice grated unfamiliarly and
she tried to clear it. 'Is—is he all right?'

The storm was definitely diminished, and seemed to
have become more a distant thrash of sound somewhere
in the darkness rather than an immediate menace, so that
Rowan heard the rasping effort of James' breathing when
he bent over his friend and laid a tentative hand on his
shoulder. René's eyes remained closed, but he licked his
lips and gave a brief slow nod.

'I'm all right.'

His voice too had the same harshness, brought on by
exhaustion and a surfeit of salt water. He spoke in French,
Rowan noticed too, which was unusual when he was with
James, but he made no move to change his position at all,
and she glanced anxiously up at James. 'I wish he'd—
just move,' she whispered, and René raised his head a
little from the ground and shook it impatiently.

'I'm exhausted, that's all,' he insisted. 'I want to rest.'

Satisfied that there was nothing seriously wrong, James
ran both hands through his dripping hair and looked around
him. There was little enough to see as far as Rowan could
tell, for they seemed to be isolated in the blackness with
only the white spume of the breakers and their own pale
faces to relieve it.

'Well, you can't rest here,' James decided with something of his more familiar manner, despite the raspingly
harsh voice. 'We'll have to move in further before we even
think of resting.'

It was possible, Rowan found after a few moments, to
make out shapes of a more dense blackness, but nothing
that was identifiable. Whether or not either of her companions knew their whereabouts, she had no idea, but her
own limited vision gave little hope of human habitation,

and in a moment of sheer panic she moved closer to James.

'Where are we?' she asked in a voice that quivered despite her efforts to steady it.

'God knows!' René heaved himself up and sat with his elbows on his knees, his head in his hands and sounding deplete of hope. 'We could be anywhere after the steering going like that and the wind taking us!'

Her heart thudded hard and in the rain-soaked blackness it was to James that she looked for reassurance, although the significance of it did not strike her as yet. 'James?'

The panic that welled in her was betrayed in the sound of her voice and when he reached out and hugged her against his reassuring strength she buried her face in the hollow of his shoulder while one large hand cradled the back of her head. 'It'll be an island of some sort,' he said with an air of confidence, 'and at least it's terra firma, we've that to be thankful for. What we have to do at this moment is find some kind of shelter, because it's useless running around in the dark and perhaps losing each other as well.'

Rowan raised her face, looking up into the craggy wet features with a trust she did not even begin to wonder at. 'Will it be inhabited?'

'That I don't know.' She sensed that he hated having to sound uncertain about it, and he tightened his arm around her for a second. 'But there has to be some kind of shelter, even if it's only rocks or trees. Now, do you feel up to moving, or shall I go alone and come back for you?'

'Oh no, don't go!' She struggled free of his arm and got to her feet, swaying for a moment when her own weakness took her by surprise and the still blustering wind almost knocked her down again. 'I'd rather come with you,' she insisted, and James reached for her hands as he got to his feet. 'I don't want to stay here, James, please!'

He was in two minds, she could see, and it was to her shame that she completely forgot about René for the moment, not taking into account the possibility of his not being up to walking any distance. It was James who reminded her when he looked down at René, still sitting with his head in his hands, and he considered for a moment.

'René?' He raised his head and seemed to realise that a decision was required of him. 'Do you feel up to coming with us?' James asked him. 'We have to find shelter somewhere away from the beach.'

He reached down when René started to rise and lent a hand, then quite automatically placed an arm around Rowan's shoulders once more. It was clear that René was undecided and he narrowed his eyes against the impenetrable darkness and the still falling rain, seeing no enticement in exchanging one discomfort for another. Then he shrugged. 'I'll come,' he said.

'Good!'

Something in the firm confidence of the reply must have touched a raw nerve, for René turned swiftly, running a hand through his hair, his voice harsh and bordering on hysteria. 'I don't know what you find to be so cheerful about!' he declared, reverting to French, and it was a second or two before James replied.

He raised his voice only as much as was necessary to be heard above the breakers. 'Will it help if I burst into tears?' he asked, then immediately smiled. It was little more than a brief glimpse of white teeth in his dark features, but to Rowan at least, it was very reassuring. 'Ah, come on, man,' he told René in his rolling Scots, 'let's go and find somewhere a bit more sheltered than this damned beach, or we may be in worse trouble before long.'

René, resigned but no more enthusiastic, allowed himself to be helped along as they battled their way up a sloping beach of shifting sand towards those darker, indefinable shapes further inland. 'How do we know we'll find any shelter?' René asked, but Rowan noticed that he spoke in

English as he most often did when he spoke to James, and she took it as a good sign.

'We don't for certain,' James replied promptly, 'but let's go and find out before we start getting pessimistic, shall we?'

Rowan, walking the other side of him, tried not to share René's determined pessimism. 'I'm sure we'll find something,' she ventured in a small, croaky voice, and just for a moment caught that gleaming slash of white teeth again.

'I'm sure we shall,' James agreed.

CHAPTER THREE

IT was both confusing and alarming to wake and to have no idea where she was, and for a moment Rowan gazed up at the unfamiliar arch of branches and vines above her head, trying to bring things to mind that she knew in her heart she would much rather forget had happened. But the traumatic events of last night had been a fact, and she closed her eyes very tightly for a moment as she tried to shut out the memory of René's anguished cry when he found the lifeboat gone. The lifeboat that her grandmother and three members of the crew had taken off into that howling storm, rather than be capsized when the yacht went down.

The sun was warm, but not as hot as she had become accustomed to in the past weeks, and she opened her eyes again and gazed up at the roof of what appeared to be a cage of branches and vines. A cage that had offered them shelter last night when they had all been too exhausted to go any further.

The shelter had no floor, only hardened earth with a carpet of rotting leaves that emitted a damp raw smell.

Close by where she lay herself, a recumbent figure turned in its sleep suddenly and revealed itself as René, and she sat up and stared across at him in mingled envy and anxiety. He still slept, apparently peacefully, but there was a slight bruise on his chin, and he still had the pallor of exhaustion in his face.

A brief check of her body found nothing physically amiss, apart from some stiffness and a few bruises that would probably soon disappear. But her long dark hair felt heavy and horribly sticky, and she ran her fingers through it and despaired of its appearance. Not that she had much time to worry about such trivia at the moment, for she realised suddenly that she and René were alone and no third sleeper lay curled up on the damp earth.

'James!' She scrambled to her feet, and got caught up in the overhead branches, murmuring impatiently as she disentangled herself, and causing even greater havoc to her untidy hair. 'James, where are you?'

René did not stir, only made a soft moaning noise in his sleep, and she did not stop, except to turn briefly and see if he woke up. When he didn't, she scrambled out through an opening in the cage of branches and stood for a moment to get her bearings. At first sight she seemed to be in the middle of an impenetrable jungle that steamed and rustled in the growing light, the sun slanting down through massive trees and drawing up last night's rain in spirals of ghostly mist.

She could hear sounds, but none that suggested another human being close by, and she stood with her hands clasped under her breast, looking all around her. Her heart thudded, so loudly that she could hear it like a faint drumming in her ears, and there were rustles and sounds all around her, but nothing to be seen.

'James!' She raised her voice, or so she thought, but it came out as little more than a croak of sound and she realised how the salt water she had swallowed during that

incredible swim, had dried and shrivelled her throat.
'James!'

She wished René would wake, but she hesitated to wake
him because of the three of them he seemed to have been
worst affected by their ordeal last night, and sleep was a
great healer. She almost wished she could have slept for
longer herself, for her head felt muzzy and she ached as
she never had before as she stood there indecisively, her
one thought at the moment to find James Fraser, wherever
he might be.

The first few steps she took made it clear that her expensive leather shoes had hardened in the sea water and
cramped her feet horribly. Only the T-bar strap over the
instep had prevented them from being lost, she suspected,
and thanked heaven for small mercies, for she did not think
she could have managed barefoot. Also the shirt and skirt
she was wearing, and which she supposed was all she now
had in the world, had become limp and sticky and chafed
her skin which was already reddened and tender.

She had never felt more wretchedly uncomfortable in
her life, and yet she could still feel thankful that she had
come through that terrifying ordeal last night more or less
unscathed. But for James Fraser she would have died, she
felt sure of it, and she wondered how she was ever going
to repay him for cursing and bullying her to such effect
through that turbulent sea last night. That was if she
could find him.

A flutter of panic shivered through her like a chill wind,
and she started forward on sheer impulse with no idea
where to go. It was steamily wet underfoot, almost marshy,
and her feet hurt in the cramping shoes, but she had no
time to worry about such things at the moment as she
dodged around vine-tangled trees searching blindly for a
clue to which way to go, hopefully calling his name as she
went.

'James!'

There was water running somewhere and instinctively she turned in that direction, though she had no idea where it might lead her. There was life too, among the trees, her senses told her so. Something that moved swiftly through the tops of the trees, making no more than a slight crackle of leaves and branches, but with watching eyes that sent trickles of cold fear along her spine, seeing, but unseen, and adding to her growing panic. Then a bird shrilled somewhere and she started nervously.

'James? James, where are you?'

She turned her head as she walked, aware of those hidden eyes following her, and blundered into someone coming in the opposite direction. Her pent up alarm gave voice suddenly in a shrill sliver of sound that was somewhere between a sob and a scream, then two arms wrapped themselves tightly around her and at once she felt the fear slip away and leave only an unbelievable sense of relief.

'James!'

He held something in his hands, she had no idea what at the moment, nor did she care as she buried her head against his shoulder and hung on tightly to him. 'Here, here now, what's all the kerfuffle about?' The familiar rolling tones murmured against her ear and warm lips touched briefly to her forehead. 'You daft wee creature,' the voice admonished, and she noticed how deep and almost sensual it sounded. 'Did you think I'd swum off and left you, then?'

Rowan clung to him, almost afraid to let go, and her heart was thudding wildly in a tangle of emotions she did not begin to understand. 'I didn't know.' Her voice was muffled and she didn't want to lift her head yet, because there was something so comforting about the intimate warmth of a bare tanned chest and the encircling arms. But James eased her away from him after a moment or two, and looked down into her face, with such warmth in his eyes that she hastily lowered her own. 'I couldn't find you,' she said in the curiously husky voice she scarcely recognised as hers. 'I—I couldn't think where you were.'

'I was scavenging breakfast.'

He held up his hands to show her what he had. In one he carried two very odd-looking fish and in the other what appeared to be a makeshift sack made from his shirt which seemed to be filled with fruit of some kind. There was a look about him that fitted into their surroundings in some curious way, and made him seem a lot less alien than Rowan felt. His formerly immaculate slacks were rolled up to the ankles and his bare feet in leather sandals, and with his naked torso he had a kind of primitive confidence that was amazingly reassuring—like the faintly crooked smile he gave her as he exhibited his finds for her approval.

'It's not the Ritz but it's edible, and we'll all feel better with a meal inside us.'

His optimism did a lot to cheer her, but it was all too raw and frightening to Rowan and she eyed the ugly fish dubiously, licking her salty lips before she spoke. 'Can we cook them?' she asked, and James shook his head at her in mild reproach.

'By some miracle I have a lighter in my pocket that still works after its dousing,' he told her, then glanced around them at the crowding trees. 'And there's no shortage of wood, as you can see, though it will mebbe be a bit damp and take some firing.' He saw her look; the wide anxiety in her eyes and the slight droop that drew down the corners of her mouth, and again he shook his head. 'Trust me, Rowan, I'll not let you starve.'

'I do trust you.'

She meant it, she knew, and she saw the way James' eyes warmed again when he looked down at her. 'Then let's go and see what we can do with these ugly brutes, shall we?' She fell into step beside him, wondering at his seeming confidence in the route he was taking through the tangle of trees and vines, and after a second or two he turned his head and looked at her. 'Is René awake yet?'

'Not yet.' She wondered if by now René was in fact

awake and beginning to think he had been deserted by
both of them. 'I thought it was best to let him sleep as long
as he could.'

'Good idea.' He seemed on the point of saying something else, but in fact it was several moments before he
spoke again. 'René isn't going to adapt very easily to our
rough and ready cuisine,' he said, and in such a tone that
it was clear he did not expect an argument.

But Rowan glanced at him from the corner of her eye,
certain she detected a hint of criticism and prepared to
defend René against it if necessary. 'I'm sure he'll be as
hungry as we are and glad of anything you've brought
us.'

His expression gave little away, but he shrugged his
broad shoulders in a way that suggested he yielded rather
than argue. 'Aye well—we'll see.'

Rowan had so far deliberately put the fate of her grandmother and the others out of her mind, but now that James
was back with them, and things were, if not back to normal, at least taking on a veneer of normality, it became
impossible to close her mind to it any longer. Passing an
anxious tongue over her dry lips, she glanced up at him,
seeking to absorb some of his confidence.

'James, I wondered—about Grand'mère, and the
others——' She shook her head, her emotions almost
choking off the words when the full realisation of what
could have happened came home to her. 'Did—could they
have had a chance, do you think?'

James stopped, and transferred the bundle of fruit to
the same hand as the two fish he carried, then he put his
free hand on her cheek as he turned to face her. The sun
beamed down on to his head and the thick tawny mane of
his hair reminded her of her grandmother's description of
him as a Leo man; thick pale lashes casting shadows on
his cheeks as he looked down at her. Lightly, almost automatically, he brushed back strands of dark hair from her

face while he spoke.

'We can only hope so, Rowan,' he said softly. 'I can't promise any more than that—I wish I could.'

'Oh, James——'

Tears welled into her eyes and there seemed nothing she could do about it, and he reached out to draw her once more to the comforting breadth of his chest. His arm held her tightly and his voice murmured close to her ear, his warm breath stirring her hair and tracing little thrills of sensation over her skin.

'Now, now,' he scolded softly. 'Don't be such a pessimist, my girl! If I know Maggie as well as I think I do, *she's* probably the one who's gone fishing and gathering fruit. You can't keep a woman like your grannie down for very long, Rowan, and you wouldn't want her to think her granddaughter was a cry-baby, would you?' Rowan shook her head silently, swallowing hard on the tears that choked her, and James bent his head briefly and kissed her mouth. It was a light, almost paternal kiss, but very reassuring for all that. 'Don't worry, little one,' he went on with every appearance of confidence, 'somebody will find us before too long and then you'll wonder what all the fuss was about.'

'You really think they will?'

James dropped another light kiss on her forehead, then turned her into the reassuring curve of his arm, drawing her along with him when he started back through the tangle of trees once more, letting her go only when the going made it impossible. 'It's pretty hard to lose yourself in this day and age,' he told her, 'and in the meantime we have an island stocked with fruit and fish. We're lucky to be alive. O.K.?'

'O.K.?' Rowan agreed, and felt suddenly as if things were perhaps not quite so bad after all.

Rowan had never eaten under such conditions before,

and in other circumstances she might have enjoyed it for the novelty. As it was she was thankful for any number of things, including the fact that she had food to eat, however unfamiliar it was. She had never eaten fish smoked over a wood fire before, but having no choice she made the best of it, telling herself that the acrid smoke of the fire, as well as her own ravenous hunger, made the slightly muddy flavour of the fish almost acceptable.

It had surprised her initially to realise what an appetite she had, and she had eaten every scrap of the portion that James had given her following it with a couple of small but very juicy oranges that did a lot to restore her palate to normal. James had even provided a drink in the form of a coconut, suitably bored with holes, whose sweet fresh milk had helped to slake the awful thirst she had. And she had not minded in the least that the milk dribbled awkwardly down her chin when she drank.

René, on the other hand, had eaten no more than a mouthful of the fish, and only very warily tried a mangolike fruit when James insisted he had something. He was obviously far from happy and not at the moment interested in making the best of their situation. His refusal to eat the fish and his suspicion of the fruit he ate reminded Rowan that James had expected something of the kind when he mentioned it earlier. He was obviously not going to adapt very easily to their enforced crude diet.

She found his attitude disturbingly petulant in the circumstances, and with the idea of encouraging him, reached across and placed a hand on his arm. Conscious of James watching her when she smiled a little tremulously. 'You should try and eat something, René,' she coaxed. 'If we're going to search for Grand'mère and the others afterwards, you should eat something first.'

'It's foul!' René declared, giving his makeshift plate a disgusted look and pushing it further away from him. 'I'm not even sure we should be eating the damned thing; it looks more like a snake than a fish and it tastes like nothing on earth!'

It was true that the fish looked very unappetising. It was a curious colour and being served up on a strip of bark it was not guaranteed to make an enjoyable meal, but it was food and it could have tasted a lot worse, Rowan felt. Also James had gone to the trouble of catching it for them, and it seemed rather ungrateful to simply turn her nose up at it. 'It was a bit—odd,' she allowed, with a glance at James, 'but it wasn't too bad really, René.'

James sat with his legs akimbo, pale lashes hiding the look in his eyes while he ate his way through one of the tiny oranges, and he glanced up only briefly, wiping juice from his lips with one big, inelegant hand. 'It's a species of mud-fish,' he told them, 'and not very palatable, I grant you. But it's edible and it's filling, and those are the most important factors at the moment. If you really object to it, René, why don't you try some more fruit? These oranges are good, aren't they Rowan?' She nodded agreement, and he went on talking in an easy conversational tone that was, to Rowan at least, comfortingly normal. 'This place must have been cultivated once, even if it isn't now. I found oranges, bananas and these mango things all growing wild, but they must have been brought here originally because they're not native. Attempts *have* been made to cultivate islands round here, then abandoned.'

René looked at him with a curiously helpless look in his eyes that to Rowan was both appealing and hard to understand in view of the number of times he had wished he could travel and live as James had. 'It isn't inhabited now, is it?' he asked, and James shrugged, giving his whole attention to the fruit he was eating.

'That's one of the things we'll find out when we've had our breakfast and cleaned ourselves up a bit,' he promised, and his gaze shifted to Rowan for a moment. 'What about you, Rowan? Do you feel up to crashing your way through what seems to be marshy jungle?' Briefly he smiled and his eyes held her uncertain gaze with a glimmer of humour in their depths that was very reassuring. 'I know all about the equality of the modern woman, but this could be rough going and I subscribe to the more old-fashioned ideas about women, especially little, dainty women who aren't cut out for this. If you'd rather stay here, I'll understand.'

Somehow she managed a smile, but Rowan could not face the prospect of his going off and leaving her behind, no matter how tough the going was, so she spoke up quickly and unhesitatingly. 'Oh no, I'd much rather come with you!' she assured him, and even though she noticed René frown she still stuck to her decision. 'I'll be all right, honestly.'

'You're sure?' James insisted, but she noticed satisfaction in the faint smile he gave her. 'René could stay with you, and you'd be quite safe.'

'No, no, I'd much rather come!'

He was pleased, she could see it, and he darted a brief glance at René before going on with his plan. It was taken for granted, she noted with no surprise, that James took the lead and they followed. 'That's settled, then,' he said. 'As soon as you two have cleaned up, we'll start looking for the others; along the shore, I think. They won't have strayed too far inland any more than we have.'

René glanced from one to the other as if he found no cause at all for optimism, and thought them slightly mad for even attempting a search. 'Do you really think you'll find them?' he asked, and Rowan caught her lower lip between her teeth. The possibility of not finding them was something she dared not think about, and she automatically looked to James to provide a more optimistic opinion.

'I don't see why not,' he told René quietly. '*We* landed up here safe and sound, and they had a boat, they stood more chance.'

'But in that——' He caught James' eye and hastily bit back what he had been going to say, glancing at Rowan when he realised the effect he was having. 'You're probably right,' he allowed, but with such lack of conviction it did nothing to reassure her at all.

'The sooner we start, the sooner we find out,' James declared, and once more injected a note of optimism into the conversation. 'While I was scouting around for something to eat, I made a discovery, incidentally; if anyone fancies a dip to freshen up, there's fresh water just back there. There's a fairly big hill goes up just behind the clearing and I'd say it's a spring from up there somewhere.'

'*Fresh* water?'

Rowan's delight was undisguised, and James had at least one enthusiastic listener. 'It's cold,' he warned, 'but it's fresh and clean and it makes you feel a whole lot better after you've dunked yourself in it. If anyone's interested in taking a cold bath I'll show you the way.'

'That's where you'd been when I came to find you?' Rowan guessed, and he nodded. She realised then why his tanned and naked torso had such a healthy glow and why it had smelled so fresh and clean when he held her in his arms for those few moments. 'Oh, it would be lovely to have a bath. I don't care whether it's hot, cold or lukewarm as long as it's clean and not salty!'

'A cold bath?' René looked horrified at the very idea, and obviously didn't understand her enthusiasm at all. 'Darling, you must be mad!'

'Mad or not,' Rowan told him, already revelling in the imagined feel of clean water flowing over her body, 'I'm going to have a bath!'

'As we're a bit short on linen,' said James, 'I'll lend you my shirt to dry yourself on afterwards.' He noted her quick frown and took a pinch of material between thumb and forefinger. 'Terry-towelling,' he pointed out. 'I found it very handy, and it soon dries in the sun.'

René very obviously didn't like the situation, nor did he care for the smile he noticed pass between them. It was quite deliberate when he inched along the ground and closed the distance between them, then placed an arm around Rowan's shoulders. His mouth again showed that hint of petulance and quite obviously he was in no mood to co-operate and make the best of things. Drawing her to him, he kissed her mouth, lightly but possessively, as if it was something he had often done before rather than a new innovation that took Rowan slightly by surprise.

'*Chérie,*' he murmured in French, Rowan noticed, as if to exclude James from what he said. 'You cannot surely mean to actually bathe in that—that river that James has found——'

'It's a pool, as a matter of fact,' James interrupted smoothly, and Rowan noticed the way his eyes gleamed. He followed René's intention quite easily, she thought, but he found it amusing rather than annoying.

'Pool or river or whatever it is,' René declared, 'you said it's cold, and I've never had a cold bath in my life! You be as spartan as you like, but I prefer something a bit more civilised!'

'René!'

It was Rowan who made the protest, while James sat still and quiet as a bronze Buddha for several seconds before he spoke again. He had, Rowan realised, the most remarkable self-control, for his eyes were neither quiet nor placid, but gleaming like ice between their pale lashes. Then he smiled.

'Och, come on, man,' he taunted softly, 'don't quake at the thought of a cold bath; it'll not hurt you! It's a bonus in a way if you think about it.'

'It's the last straw!' René retorted.

'Not by a long way, my friend!' James argued, and there was an edge of hardness on his voice. 'You've a hell of a lot

more straws to put up with before you get to the last one,
believe me!'

Rowan could feel the tension like a tangible thing between them and she hastened to pour oil on to troubled
water if it was all possible. 'We could be a lot worse off,' she
assured René soothingly. 'After all, we've had food and
drink, it could be a lot worse.' Again the possible fate of
her grandmother and the others was brought forcibly to
mind, and she looked down at the trembling hands in her
lap, her lip caught between her teeth. 'I only hope Grand'-
mère is faring as well as we are.'

Not altogether surprisingly, it was James' big hand that
was pressed consolingly over hers, and she looked at him
mistily. 'Maggie will be all right,' he insisted, 'take my
word, Rowan.' He stood up, purposeful and confident in
the damp steamy clearing, and reached down his hands to
her. Pulling her swiftly to her feet, he held her hands for a
moment longer. 'Are you taking first bath?' he asked, and
Rowan noticed the swift upward jerk of René's head.

'I don't know.' She glanced down at him, hugging his
knees and determinedly pessimistic. 'Shall I go first, René?'

His lip was thrust out and his eyes looked darkly unhappy, and it was impossible not to sympathise with him
to some degree. He was so much out of his element, so
much less able to cope than the good friend whom he had
so often claimed to envy. But there was something other
than his own discomfort troubling him at the moment,
Rowan thought, and noticed how he darted his glance
between her and James.

'Taking a cold bath is bad enough,' he said after a second
or two, 'but I draw the line at you taking it with James in
attendance!'

It was a moment before Rowan fully understood the
implication, and when she did she stared at him indig-
nantly. Colour warmed her cheeks and her eyes gleamed
with the beginnings of temper, but before she could

give vent to her indignation James had already taken up the challenge, looking at René from below his heavy and deceptively lazy-looking lids.

'You're daft, man,' he told him flatly and without emotion. 'I'm going with Rowan to show her where the pool is and as far as I'm concerned that's it. Of course if Rowan wants it another way, then I'm more than willing to oblige, naturally.'

'You——'

René scrambled to his feet, his face distorted in a way that completely ruined his good looks. He was shaking with anger and Rowan for once understood his fury and blamed James for what he must have known would be a provocative statement.

'Tell him, Rowan!' René sent her a swift agonised look of appeal. 'Tell him you don't want him hanging around you! Better still, tell him you don't want to go to his damned pool! Tell him, Rowan!'

So suddenly plunged into a scene that was completely alien to her, Rowan was confused. She found it hard to believe it was really happening, and to help steady her, to give her hands something to do, she bent and retrieved James' shirt from the ground, brushing off the clinging leaves and fragments of damp earth that clung to it.

'I think you're both behaving badly if you want to know!' she declared in as firm a voice as she was capable of in the circumstances. 'You—neither of you know me very well if you imagine I'd even consider taking a bath just to provide your—entertainment! If I knew where the pool was I'd go on my own; as it is I need James to show me where it is. After that he can go as far away as possible while I take my bath, and stay away until I'm dressed again!'

James showed neither disappointment nor surprise at her declaration, but there was a look in his eyes that Rowan found oddly disturbing and she blinked at him in confusion when he held out his hand. 'I'll let you borrow my shirt,' he told her, 'but until you need it I might as well put it on again.' She looked at the towelling shirt in her hand somewhat dazedly for a moment. 'You don't mind, do you?'

'Oh no, of course not—I'm sorry!'

He took the shirt from her and pulled it on, then cast René a brief speculative glance before looking back at Rowan. 'Well,' he said, 'are you still interested in taking that bath?'

'Yes.' She spared René only a brief look, unwilling to be deterred. 'Yes, of course.'

'Then let's go,' James said briskly. 'We've a search party to get under way, and I'm sure René will decide to have that bath after all.'

René said nothing, only looked on with that same unhappy and resentful gaze while James slipped a hand under her arm and drew her along with him. He set such a pace that Rowan found it too hard to maintain, especially in such heat, and they were barely out of sight of their temporary shelter when she brought them to a halt, meeting James' look of enquiry with a reproachful challenge.

'Don't walk so fast, James; I've no intention of running all the way there!'

His hand was still curved about her arm and his long fingers felt firm and cool on her skin, and when he looked down at her there was only a suggestion of amusement in his eyes. 'Of course not,' he allowed. 'I'm sorry, I didn't realise.'

Standing as they were, close together among the crowding, vine-tangled trees, it struck Rowan that there was a curious kind of intimacy in the situation. Her heart was racing, but that could quite easily be the effect of hurrying so much in the hot and humid atmosphere, and the colour that warmed her cheeks could be attributed to the same cause. And yet somehow Rowan had the strangest feeling that both were due more to the look she noticed in

the ice-blue eyes that gazed at her in a way she did not remember having seen before.

Then James let go her arm and instead stretched out a
hand for her to take, and when she hesitated, crooked the
long fingers invitingly. 'I just forgot how little you are,'
he promised with a softness in his voice that was alarmingly
affecting. 'Come on, Rowan, I'll not make you hurry too
much, I promise.' One brow arched upward and the light
eyes were fixed on her unwaveringly. 'You trust me, don't
you?' he asked.

In fact it rather surprised Rowan to realise just how
much she did trust him, and after only a brief hesitation
she put her hand into his. But the moment of contact was
so pleasurable that it startled her for a moment and set
the blood racing swiftly through her veins, heightening
her already warm colour. James noticed it, of course, and
he smiled at her in a way that pulled his mouth down
slightly at its corners.

'You *do* trust me, don't you, Rowan?'

'Yes.' She glanced up at him from the corner of her
eye, accepting the challenge as he would expect her to. 'If
you mean do I trust you not to play Peeping Tom while I
have my bath; I shouldn't have come with you otherwise.'

'René too?'

He asked the question in such a way that it aroused inexplicable suspicions, and she twisted her head around
quickly to look at him again. It was hard to judge how far
his own trust of René went, and she wondered for the first
time just how close their friendship really was. They enjoyed one another's company and they had had some good
times together, but always in circumstances far removed
from the present ones. In this hot, alien world James was
to some extent in his element, while René was like a fish
out of water. Here they did not meet on equal terms, but
where James had a distinct advantage.

'I trust René too,' she told him, and the angle of her

chin dared him to doubt it; a dare that earned a hard
squeeze from the enfolding fingers. 'Anyway,' she added
a little breathlessly, 'I don't have much option if I'm to
get my bath, do I?'

'Not a lot,' James agreed with bland frankness, and used
one hand to push a way through a thick tangle of vines.

It wasn't long before Rowan recognised the sound of
running water and instinctively glanced up at her com-
panion. James nodded, smiling faintly, and only moments
later he broke a way through into a small clearing, marshy
underfoot as the whole island seemed to be, but open to
the sky and as a result even hotter. Despite the higher
temperature, it was such a blessing to be free of the crowding jungle for a few moments that Rowan heaved a sigh
of relief.

'An open space!' she breathed, closing her eyes against
the bright hot sun. 'Ooh, how I'm beginning to hate that
jungle of trees!'

'Already?' James taunted, and she turned to him defensively.

'I feel crowded in,' she explained. 'And there are—
things that watch you.'

'Things?' He obviously found her complaint cause for
amusement, for he was smiling in that faintly mocking
way she was beginning to recognise. 'What kind of things,
for heaven's sake, you daft wee creature?'

She remembered him using that expression once before,
but in this instance disliked its suggestion of patronage.
'You know what I mean,' she insisted, frowning at him. 'I've
heard things moving in the tops of the trees and screeches
—awful screeches. And when I came to look for you
earlier on, I felt—I'm *sure* someone or something was
watching me; I could feel eyes on me.'

'You've a great imagination!' Remembering made her
less willing to be left alone, even to safeguard her privacy,
and she started visibly when James put a hand to her

cheek and lightly smoothed his long fingers over her salt-caked skin. 'Och, Rowan, who do you think is going to hurt you here? The screeches you heard were birds, most likely parakeets, they kick up a hell of a din, and it was mebbe their beady eyes you felt on you. Or lizards, harmless and more scared of you than you are of them. The only things likely to give you a nip are the mosquitoes, and they'll not kill you.'

'All right, I'm a baby!' She admitted it in a small, cross voice that reproached him for his lack of understanding, although she did not really believe he was lacking in feeling. 'What about snakes?' The thought struck her with sudden horror, for she had a dread of reptiles and did not care about being branded a coward for showing it. 'There might be snakes here, James, you don't know!'

'I don't know,' James agreed with studied frankness. 'But you've a choice, Rowan, of taking a nice cold refreshing bath, or of staying in your present state of salty stickiness, and unless I personally stand guard I can't guarantee you complete immunity from the local wildlife.'

'I—I know.'

The touch of his hand on her cheek was light and almost hypnotic, a caress that she found comforting rather than erotic. 'Then make up your mind, little girl,' he told her softly, and Rowan did not even object to the name he called her.

The water came down a gradual slope from somewhere among the trees and its gentle trickle was somehow unexpected, for it had sounded like a deluge when she heard it from a distance. Bubbling and sparkling, it flowed over a smooth boulder, no more than a metre high, into a narrow pool, before disappearing among the trees again.

'It doesn't even taste slightly of salt,' James told her, noticing how she eyed the water avidly, 'so it must be well back from the highest tide at its outlet. It comes down from that hill you can see up there. I climbed up a little way when I was out foraging, and there's nothing but jungle until you come to a narrow strip of shoulder-high grass, then more of this.'

'You did all that before I got up?' she asked, and James laughed.

'I'm one of those annoying people who always gets up early,' he said. 'And the beds here aren't exactly interior sprung, are they?' He shook his head, dismissing facetiousness for a more serious report. 'As far as I could tell from the height I went to, we're near one end of the island, but there's a hell of a lot more of it stretching out in the other direction; all of it jungle as far as I can see.'

'And that's what we have to get through to find Grand'-mère?'

'It's very possible,' said James, and obviously disliked having to admit it. 'With luck we can go along the beach, which will be much easier going, but quite often in terrain like this the trees come right down to the tideline.'

'They couldn't be this end—like we are?'

He shook his head, although she thought he did so regretfully. 'The way the tide brought us in makes it unlikely. They're almost certainly at the other end of the island or, let's hope, part way along it.'

Somehow she managed a faint smile, though she wasn't quite sure how. 'I'm grateful that you don't treat me like a baby,' she told him in a small husky voice. 'I'd rather you were honest with me, James.'

A hand slid beneath her chin and just briefly his lips brushed hers. 'I'm sorry, little one,' he murmured. 'I promise I'll do my very best to get you out of this.' He glanced at the shimmering pool behind her and it was as if he put on a mask when he resumed his air of briskness. 'In the meantime you'd better have that bath you need so much, hadn't you?'

Perhaps it was the thought of being left completely alone in surroundings she mistrusted that made her suddenly so nervous, but it was almost compulsive when she yielded to her own weakness. 'Where will you be?' she ventured, and knew he wouldn't misunderstand her.

'Not too far away that I shan't hear you yell,' he promised, and ran his fingers down in to the hollow of her throat. 'O.K.?' She nodded and he grasped his shirt hem and stripped it off in one swift move, handing it to her with a wry grin. 'Lucky I was wearing a towelling shirt, wasn't it? The skeeters will have to make a meal of me while you make use of it, then spread it out to dry for René when you've finished.'

Rowan glanced at his broad, sun-tanned torso, then hastily looked away again, for there was something alarmingly disturbing about him in the present situation. 'You should really keep it on,' she told him, in a voice that was not quite steady, and once more that wide, expressive and slightly mocking mouth crooked into a smile.

'They don't bother me too much as a rule,' he told her. 'And it's all we have to use as a towel, so there's no alternative. I'll be all right, Rowan, don't you worry about me, you just enjoy your bath, O.K.?'

He waited for her brief but doubtful nod, then laughed suddenly and without warning bent his head and very thoroughly kissed her mouth. Immediately he walked off, back into the concealing trees, and as she watched him go for a moment, Rowan fought hard against an instinct that prompted her to call him back. Instead she watched the last sight of his long lean shape, then turned and started to take off the few clothes she was wearing.

It was cold, stunningly cold at first, but after a second or two the water felt silky and smooth and incredibly refreshing, so that she ducked her head as well and rinsed the salt from her hair, wringing it out while she stood breast-high in the pool. She hesitated briefly before she climbed out, conscious again of watching eyes and feeling the same nervous reaction, even though she had James' assurance that it was most likely the bird population that kept watch on her.

Drying herself on James' shirt was only half successful, but it took off most of the water, and the sun soon dried the rest, because it was much hotter in the little clearing. Her clothes, which she had hastily rinsed out, were almost dry when she put them on again, and she had to admit to feeling much fresher and better able to cope with anything that came along. A long cool drink had been wonderfully refreshing too.

She was shrugging into her shirt when something caught her eye suddenly and she first gasped, then let out a full-throated scream of terror. There was no doubt in her mind at all that the eyes that watched her from the density of the nearby bushes were human, and her reaction had been automatic. Had the eyes been light blue and recognisable her response would have been angry embarrassment, for she would have identified them easily enough, but they were dark and glowing with an expression she shrank from because it was somehow vaguely menacing.

Her first thought was that some island inhabitant had discovered her, and her heart raced wildly while she stood rooted in fear, waiting for James to appear as he had promised. She stared in blank disbelief when the bushes parted and a body thrust through into the clearing; not a dark-skinned islander, but René, looking sheepishly anxious, and his eyes no longer glowing in that curiously menacing way.

Anger followed swiftly on fear as a natural reaction, and she turned on him furiously, making far more of his having been watching her than she would normally have done. 'How *dare* you?' she stormed at him. 'How dare you sneak behind the bushes and watch me like some—some nasty little voyeur!'

'Rowan!' René reached for her hands and held them tightly, but Rowan felt naked and horribly vulnerable, so that she struggled to free herself as anxiously as René fought to retain his hold on her. 'Rowan, please listen to me! I haven't been watching; I've only just come, I——'

James' sudden appearance was as dramatic as René's had been, and much more impressive. He came across the little clearing in long loping strides that gave him the slightly menacing look of a big cat; a lion of a man with his mane of tawny-gold hair, and alarmingly disturbing. Rowan felt a curious elation at the sight of him and did not understand her own reaction; but she felt dismay too because she had brought him on a fool's errand.

'James!'

She whispered his name while she pulled her hands free of René's suddenly nerveless grip. James switched his ice-blue gaze from one to the other, clearly in two minds about the reason for her cry for help. 'Mebbe I needn't have bothered after all,' he suggested, and Rowan detected a curious and unfamiliar flatness in his voice.

René was quite obviously both puzzled and annoyed by his sudden appearance, and he was frowning when he looked down again at Rowan's flushed face and evasive eyes. 'You couldn't have been very far away,' he said to James, making no attempt to disguise his suspicion. 'I understood you to say you were going to bring Rowan here and then leave her alone to have her bath.'

James' eyes narrowed, the heavy lids drooping almost sleepily. 'I left the choice to Rowan herself, if I remember correctly,' he drawled in his soft burr. 'As it happened she asked me to stay close by in case she shouted for help. Do you suppose she had an idea you might turn up unexpectedly?' he added with a faint smile, and René flushed angrily.

In the event it was Rowan who answered him, hastily and a little breathlessly. 'You know it wasn't anything like that, James,' she reproached him. 'It was—snakes and things like that I was afraid of.'

'Instead it was René,' James reminded her, and clearly would not be satisfied until it was explained to him, something Rowan was loath to do.

She did not relish the idea of telling him that her first intimation of René's presence had been a glimpse of glowing dark eyes watching her from the thickness of the bushes. There was no way of making that sound like an innocent accident, so she veered a little from the whole truth, wondering why she hated so much deceiving him, however mildly.

'I—I heard him coming and it scared me,' she explained, and caught a glimpse of René's surprised reaction from the corner of her eye. 'You know how jumpy I was, James, and hearing him——' She spread her hands in a gesture of appeal. 'I just screamed automatically; I'm sorry.'

'I see,' he murmured, and his eyes strayed for a moment to the gaping front of her shirt, so that she quickly gathered it into slightly unsteady fingers. 'But still,' he went on, 'you won't need me now you have René, will you? Unless you'd like me to guide you back to our—for want of a better name—camp?'

'There's no need!' René's voice almost cut him short, and he curved a disturbingly possessive hand over her arm so that Rowan very nearly brushed it away instinctively. 'I know the way back,' René went on, and there was a note of satisfaction in the way he said it that was unmistakable. 'You've no need to wait, James.'

'Rowan?'

The soft-voiced enquiry ignored his dismissal, and she noticed how René's colour rose while the fingers on her arm tightened their grip almost cruelly. 'I've told you I can find the way back,' he insisted, and Rowan had the discomforting sensation of being torn between the two of them. 'You tell him, Rowan.'

It was not in her nature to obey instinctively, and especially an instruction spoken in that peremptory tone,

but it was her need to prevent bad blood growing between
the two men that decided her. Her inclination was to go
with James because he certainly knew the way back; on
the other hand René would make far more fuss if she
deserted him than James would.

'I think I could find my way back,' she said, the tone
of her voice begging him to understand her reasons, and
James regarded her steadily for a second.

'You're sure?'

'She won't need to find her own way back,' René interrupted shortly. '*I'll* bring her!'

'After you've had your bath?'

The implication was unmistakable, and René looked both
sheepish and annoyed. 'All right!' he declared flatly. 'I'll
just have a moment with my girl, on our own if you don't
mind, then I'll have my bath. Rowan can wait in the wings;
like you did,' he added with undisguised malice.

'Or I can find my own way back,' Rowan hastened to add,
and laughed as she sought to ease the tension a little. 'If
I'm not back in an hour, James, you'd better come looking
for me!'

But for once James was not seeing the funny side of anything and she met the gravity of his eyes uneasily. 'I'll have
quite enough to think about organising a search for your
grannie and the others,' he reminded her, and to Rowan
the reminder was unnecessarily harsh in the circumstances.
'And I've certainly no wish to stay and play gooseberry, so
I'll leave you to it.'

He turned away and was lost from sight in the surrounding jungle again before Rowan had time to recover her
breath, and she saw him disappear with much less satisfaction than René did. He seemingly saw himself as having
won some kind of a victory, and he took both her hands
in his again and smiled down at her with glowingly dark
blue eyes.

'I knew you wouldn't desert me,' he told her with a confi-

dence that somehow grated on her nerves. 'Oh, my lovely,
sweet Rowan, at last I have you all to myself!' He bent his
head and pressed his lips very lightly on to hers, then let
his glance plunge to the open front of her shirt. 'Oh, my
love!' He nuzzled her neck, murmuring in her ear and
brushing her skin with his lips, lightly and erotically. But
to Rowan this was not the time, she had too much else on
her mind.

'Please, René, this isn't the time or the place!'

She fought the enfolding arms without really knowing
why she was so anxious to be free of him. During the
weeks aboard the *Belle o' Dunoon* she had never doubted
that René found her attractive, just as she did him, but
somehow this morning there was a new kind of brashness
in his manner that suggested he saw less need to restrain
himself now that she was no longer under the eye of her
grandmother.

'Rowan, you don't know how much I've longed for us to
be together like this.' He glanced around as if he had
actually forgotten where they were, and shook his head.
'Well, perhaps not like this; but with no one to see us. And
you know how I feel about you, Rowan, I've told you, that
last evening before all this happened, and now——'

'*No*, René, I—I can't think about things like that at
the moment! Surely you realise that; we have to find
Grand'mère, that's what matters most to me right now.'

He kissed her mouth, but it was a brash, hard kiss that
was merely a way of silencing her, and she struggled more
determinedly than ever to free herself. 'I love you, Rowan!'
His voice was harsh and rasping. 'I believe you love me,
only you don't realise it yet!' He kissed her again, clasping
her tightly and murmuring all the time. 'You don't realise
it yet, but I'll persuade you!' His eyes gleamed and he
pressed his mouth to hers again in a more lingering caress,
smoothing a hand over her back while he kissed her. 'Oh,
my Rowan, how I shall enjoy persuading you!' He laughed

a little wildly. 'It must surely be fate that threw us together like this!'

Rowan thought of her grandmother and the rest of the crew, of their own precarious position, stranded on an island heaven knew where, and she could not believe he was thinking very straight. 'René, we're shipwrecked! We don't even know where we are for sure, and the rest of our party are missing; how can you talk as if we're—we're on holiday in the Bahamas?'

He looked faintly petulant, as if he resented the reminder, then he let her go while he stripped off his shirt. 'That's James' responsibility,' he told her. 'The yacht was his and he's responsible for our safety, to my way of thinking.'

'Oh no!' His attitude seemed scarcely credible, and she looked at him with a doubting darkness in her grey eyes. 'René, that simply isn't fair and you know it. Besides, James can't do everything, we have to help!'

'I don't see how.' The petulant thrust of his lip showed how much he disliked her reaction; suggested that he expected her to share his feeling that James was to blame in some way for their being wrecked. 'James knows how to survive in this wretchedly uncomfortable climate. I don't, I hate it! All this steamy heat and the bugs—ugh! I hate looking like a scarecrow and feeling worse, but he thrives on it; he's done it all before. This—this close to the earth living is no new experience for him, that's why he's able to come up with things to eat, revolting as some of it is, and why he's able to seem bolder and braver than the rest of us! He doesn't have to adapt, he's used to it!'

Some of what he said was undoubtedly true, but Rowan found most of the declaration less than just. So many times René had expressed his envy of James' more adventurous way of life, but now that he had been plunged into it he obviously took a much less enthusiastic view. Also she thought she detected a note of hysteria in his voice, just as she had last night at the height of the storm.

Rowan thought of her grandmother and longed for the re-assurance of that confident, bubblingly optimistic presence as she never had before. She felt lost and scared and in need of a boost for her own wavering morale, not to be made responsible for René's. Had it not been that she could count on James being there to depend on if she needed him, she felt sure she would have sunk into despair herself.

'You've said often enough that you wished you could go on the kind of trips James goes on,' she reminded René in the hope of injecting him with a little optimism. 'Now is your chance, René.'

'I never thought it would happen!' René objected, as if she should have realised and understood that, and Rowan sighed inwardly.

'Well, it's just as well James is used to it,' she told him, hoping her voice did not betray how she was feeling. 'We're going to need him if we're ever going to survive in this jungle, and I for one am glad he's with us.'

'Because he can get us out of this?'

She looked up quickly, then nodded, thinking she followed his meaning. 'Of course.'

'Of course,' René echoed. 'You don't have much time for him otherwise, do you?'

Rowan preferred not to answer that. 'I'm going to find James now,' she told him, and turned away when he reached for her hands again, keeping out of his reach. 'You'd better not be too long having your bath either,' she added firmly. 'I shan't be happy until I know what's happened to Grand'mère.'

'Rowan!' She turned only reluctantly and steeled herself, against any plea to stay with him, although it was very hard not to be touched by the look in his eyes as he spread his hands in a gesture of helplessness. 'I'm sorry; I know how you must be worried about your *grand'mère*.'

It was hard to feel at odds with him for very long, and

Rowan managed a faint smile, clinging to the optimism that James had tried to instil into her. 'We'll find her,' she said, and went off to look for James.

CHAPTER FOUR

IT was well on towards evening, and Rowan wondered how much longer she could go without dropping from sheer exhaustion. It wasn't distance that made the going so hard, but the unending battle with the terrain; the interminable jungle that made every step an effort and required them to expend energy they could ill afford in such sweltering heat.

Their initial hope of being able to follow the coast had been abandoned right at the beginning because, apart from the small sandy cove they had fetched up on during the storm the night before, the rampant trees and vines grew right down to the water's edge. Thick, steamily hot and almost impenetrable, it gave them no choice but to make their way through it if they were to go anywhere at all.

Without even a sizeable knife to aid them, it came down to tearing the clinging vines and tangled undergrowth apart with their bare hands, and progress was not only gruelling but maddeningly slow. It was the kind of climate Rowan had never experienced before, and the relentless heat and cloying marsh sapped her energy alarmingly. Only James, with the benefit of past experiences, she supposed, seemed to accept the conditions as inevitable, and even he was tiring.

René complained incessantly and at length, more so because James had made it quite clear that he expected him to move slightly ahead with him, clearing the way and leaving Rowan a pace or two in the rear with the advantage of

having comparatively little to do but follow. James worked
steadily and with a grim determination, mostly in silence
and just occasionally glancing back at her to raise an enquiring brow; acknowledging her brief nod of assurance
with a ghost of a smile.

They had been going for hours, pausing only briefly
occasionally to rest, and once to eat the fruit James had
again provided, just as he had at breakfast time. René,
Rowan guessed, would have long since given up, as she
would have done herself, had not James kept them both
going with the same relentless determination he had shown
last night during the storm. But for all their efforts they
had seen nothing so far to suggest that anyone else had
come ashore, and Rowan's growing conviction that her
grandmother had perished added to her despair.

She had long since given up trying to take an active
part in the search, and merely followed the broad back in a
sweat-stained shirt that moved inexorably ahead of her.
Perspiration trickled down her back and made her shirt
stick to her like a second skin, and she felt that if she did
not soon rest again she would drop, her legs ached so
much.

James, she thought, had been grateful for the way she
had borne the discomfort so far, but very soon she would
have to let him know how she was feeling. The jungle
enclosed them completely, the only way out being into the
sea, and she was beginning to feel horribly claustrophobic.
She longed to be able to move without coming up against
rampant vines or towering tree trunks, and to tread on
ground that did not steam and squelch at every step. Most
of all she longed to sit down.

It was almost like an answer to a prayer when her eyes
lit on a piece of broken tree that leaned drunkenly between
two of its neighbours, for although it was thin and probably
rotten, it offered a resting place even if for only a short time,
and she moved across towards it as she called out, 'James!'

He turned swiftly and she thought he called something, but already the seemingly solid ground was giving way under her feet, and she heard René's anguished cry as she slid downward into a dark slimy bog that sucked at her body with the obscene hunger of a beast. Too stunned for a moment to make any sound herself, she began to struggle when realisation dawned at last, her frantic scrabbling making matters worse.

'Keep still, Rowan!'

James' voice thundered at her while he moved quickly across the patch of comparatively solid ground to her, and she obeyed instinctively. The slimy mud oozed all around her and she imagined all manner of creatures squirming and slithering in its primeval depths, so that she gasped and shook her head at the imagined horrors as she fought down the panic that churned inside her.

Reaching up her arms, she sobbed with relief when James' strong fingers closed hard around her wrists and held on, but his own position was precarious, balanced as he was at the very edge of the bog. He hung on grimly, glancing briefly over his shoulder at René who, since that first despairing cry, seemed rooted to the spot, then exploded impatiently:

'Give me a hand for God's sake, man!'

There was something reassuringly firm about the command that briefly muted the thudding urgency of her own heartbeat, and René seemed galvanised into action suddenly, as if the goad had been a physical one. He moved up beside James and grasped her other wrist, and between them it was only a matter of seconds before she was pulled free. She was on her knees for a couple of seconds, scarcely believing she was breathing, then a pair of large hands pulled her up and she was clasped in a bear-hug that almost squeezed the remaining breath out of her.

'Rowan!' Covered in mud from the shoulders down, she leaned her whole weight against James, breathing hard and too tired to care about anything any more, unaware of the soft, small moaning sound she made as she clung to him tightly and closed her eyes. 'Rowan, ssh now, you're all right! It's all over and you're all right.'

Thankful yet again for those comforting arms, Rowan eased her tired body gratefully against the lean reassuring length of him, aching so much and so limp with tiredness that she thought she could never face walking again through that interminable jungle. Then something pricked the skin of her back and the horror was still too recent for her to ignore it, even with James' arms around her; she cried out in fear.

She suspected everything about the steaming in-hospitality of the jungle and she was at the end of her endurance or she would never have reacted as wildly as she did. Writhing back and forth, she tried to reach behind her, clawing at the clinging wet shirt helplessly, her eyes blank with unbelieving horror, her nails tearing the thin fabric.

'There's something on my back! I felt it; something— ugh! Get it off, *please* get it off me!'

'That's enough!' James' quiet firm voice again brought her from the verge of panic and he clasped an arm across the back of her neck, pressing her face to his shoulder while he put a hand in the neck of her shirt and ripped the already torn fabric from top to bottom, pulling the two halves apart. 'Keep still; quite still!'

She obeyed the command without question, but her whole body was shaking and shivering uncontrollably when he pulled something forcibly from the skin of her back, and crushed it underfoot with a ferocity that was almost primitive. Exhausted and terrified, Rowan yielded to tears at last, clinging to James while she sobbed out her misery, her face buried in the hollow of his shoulder and her cheek pressed to his sweat-soaked shirt. René was forgotten for the moment, and she and James were the only two people in a hostile and frightening world.

'All right, take it easy now, Rowan.' A big hand smoothed gently over her bedraggled hair while his chin rested lightly on the top of her head. A soothing process that went on until her sobs gradually diminished and James eased her away from him, looking down into her tear-stained face. For the moment neither of them even looked at René, and perhaps it was he who was most conscious of the fact that the gap between her and James allowed the remnants of her shirt to fall away, leaving her virtually naked. 'O.K.?' James asked, and it was hard to read exactly what went on behind those heavy-lidded eyes.

But Rowan got the impression of gentleness and she nodded, brushing a hand across her eyes and leaving a smear of mud in the process. 'Yes. Yes, I think so—thank you.'

'Good!' He gave her a faint smile. 'But don't rub those dirty hands on your face; it's the only part of you that isn't mucky so far.' He glanced down very briefly at the space between them and seemed to realise for the first time that he had literally torn her shirt to shreds, and he pulled a face. 'You'll need another shirt too, won't you?'

Somehow having it brought to her notice made Rowan feel incredibly vulnerable and she put her hands over her breasts to hold what little covering remained firmly in place, while she carefully avoided his eyes. It was when James stepped back a pace, presumably to remedy the situation, that she caught sight of René and noticed that he looked morose and even more petulantly unhappy than before. For a moment she felt a qualm of conscience for having forgotten him, however briefly.

Whether or not René would have eventually offered his own shirt was hard to say, but in the event James had already stripped off the frankly grubby towelling shirt that had served them in another capacity earlier, and handed it to her. 'I don't know what we'd have done without this,

do you?' he asked, and he sounded so blessedly normal that
for some reason she could not comprehend, Rowan felt like
crying again.

Instead she swallowed hard and made an attempt to
match his mood, although not altogether successfully.
'What are you going to do if I have it?' she asked, and a
faint smile once more flitted briefly across James' face,
giving warmth to the icy-blue eyes, and touching her once
more with that spark of optimism.

'Well, let's say that if we meet a wandering missionary
I'm much less likely to shock him by going about topless
than you would,' said James. 'And I'll manage, don't worry.
It's mebbe not as fresh and clean as you'd like, but at least
you'll be covered where it matters.'

The soft rolling tones had an incredibly soothing effect
and just briefly Rowan raised her eyes and looked at him;
all manner of strange sensations stirring in her as she
clutched the soiled, damp shirt to her breast. 'Thank you,
James.'

'Now turn your back while she changes into it!' René's
voice, sharp with fatigue and dislike, brought him to her
notice again, and Rowan felt an overwhelming pity for him
suddenly. He was so completely out of his element, and
for all the times he had expressed envy for James' way of
life, he could surely not have expected it to be anything
like the present situation. 'You heard me!' he insisted, and
James, after a brief study of his pale, streaming face,
shrugged his shoulders and did as he demanded.

'As you say,' he agreed, and with a quiet acceptance that
could only have maddened René in his present mood.

'Did you forget I was here?' he challenged, and Rowan
noticed that he had so far made no attempt to turn away
himself. 'My God!' he went on, addressing James' broad
back. 'I'm seeing you in your true colours for the first
time, and I'm not very impressed with what I see!'

'René.' James sounded not only resigned but unutterably

tired too, as he tried to reason with someone he had always until now known and liked as a close friend. He too
must be realising that he knew the man within less well
than he thought, but he was making allowances. 'We're
all dog-tired and feeling like hell, I know, but is there any
need——'

'Yes, there's need!' René declared, cutting him short.
'You've been taking the lead, acting the big man and making Rowan more and more dependent on you ever since we
went overboard last night, and I've just about had enough
of it!'

'You want to be leader?'

There was unmistakable mockery as well as impatience in
the question and René's pale, beaded cheeks flushed, un-
certainty making him back from the challenge. 'All I want
is for you to stop taking Madame de Clare's opinion of you
as a—lion man, literally!'

'Oh, don't be a fool!' snapped James, and Rowan felt
like echoing his exasperation, but her intervention could
only make matters worse, especially if she supported him.
James was shaking his head slowly, obviously not prepared
to oblige by quarrelling with him. 'This really is a ridicu-
lous situation when you think about it—standing in the
middle of nowhere, not even knowing the name of the
island we're on, and arguing like two schoolboys!'

'I want this settled before we go any further!' René was
adamant, his blue eyes gleaming resentment, petulantly
jealous and far more like the schoolboy James had desig-
nated them than James himself. 'Rowan is *my* girl; *mine*,
is that clear?'

'Oh, for God's sake!' James heaved a sigh, running
his hands through his hair as he turned his head and looked
at him, and Rowan noticed how tiredness showed in fine
lines at the corners of his mouth and eyes. 'We've got
enough to contend with, René, fighting this blasted terrain
without fighting one another! I'm not trying to steal your

girl; I don't think Rowan's the kind of girl who's easily stolen anyway. I just happen to be here, and I know what to do in this kind of situation better than you do; I'm a shoulder to cry on, that's all.' He caught sight of Rowan's mud-streaked face and anxious eyes as she stood hugging his shirt tightly to her breast, and he shook his head. 'Oh, let the girl have some privacy while she makes herself decent,' he said, as if his patience was exhausted. 'Turn around and let her get dressed!'

'*I* don't have to!' René informed him, without consulting Rowan's opinion, and James turned again and faced him, fixing him with a steady, ice-blue gaze that would have quelled a much bolder spirit than René.

'I don't intend arguing about it,' he said in the dangerously quiet voice Rowan had heard before. 'You turn your back or I'll heave you into that swamp to cool down— understood?'

René was angry, but he must have recognised the fact that without James they probably wouldn't even survive. Nevertheless he made no immediate attempt to turn around, and after a second or two James made a move towards him. At once he turned, his hands thrust into his pockets, and his shoulders hunched. James had referred to himself as just a shoulder to cry on, but to Rowan he was their only hope, and she thought he knew that perfectly well. Just before he turned his back she met his eyes for a second and caught the fleeting glimpse of a smile.

'Hurry up and get dressed,' he told her. 'I'd like to think we can find somewhere a bit more comfortable than this to spend the night.'

He was, Rowan decided, still very firmly in charge, and she thanked heaven for it.

In fact the clearing they eventually spent the night in was no better than the one they had found last night in the storm. Whatever the drawbacks, however, they had slept from sheer exhaustion, with René carefully placing himself between Rowan and James. When she woke the following morning the circumstances were almost uncannily the same as yesterday, for René lay quite close by, still sleeping, and James was gone.

Just as she had the previous morning, Rowan went in search of him, leaving René still asleep and making her way through the tangle of undergrowth. It gave her a curious sense of satisfaction to realise that she could now recognise and follow a trail by signs like broken branches and vines, and the impression of James' sandalled feet in the marsh mud. The screeching of the birds frightened her less this morning too, though she glanced up every so often, aware of the branches overhead that shivered in the morning sun with the passing of countless wings.

She would never become used to such conditions, but her ability to adapt as well as she had surprised her. It would have been much more comfortable if her shoes had not soaked and hardened, but it was better than going barefoot, and James' shirt was, if anything, more comfortable than her own had been. It was loose and allowed what cool air there was to get to her skin, but of course it was too big and the sleeves began half-way to her elbows and the bottom reached below her hips. James Fraser was a big man.

'Rowan!'

She turned quickly, in no doubt who was calling her, and smiling when she saw James standing just a short distance away, obviously expecting her to come to him. Whether or not he saw himself as simply a shoulder to cry on when she needed one, she always felt so incredibly pleased to see him that it sometimes surprised her. Treading carefully, after yesterday's experience, she made her way across to him.

'I had a feeling you might come looking for me again,' he told her, and something in the light blue eyes stirred a responsive chord in her emotions. He thrust his big, empty hands in front of her. 'I haven't found us any breakfast yet, but I've some news you'll be glad to hear.'

Rowan stared up at him, not daring to jump to conclusions. 'You mean you——' She pressed both hands to her mouth and gazed at him with eyes that suddenly brimmed with tears; whether of relief or dread, she didn't know.

'I've found the boat,' he said. 'It's pulled up among the trees about twenty-five yards in that direction.' He jerked his head vaguely at the steaming dark jungle to his left, watching her face.

Her heart thudded so hard Rowan felt almost as if she had stopped breathing for a moment or two. Her throat felt dry and her hands were trembling as she tried to assume some of his coolness. 'Is—I mean, is there any sign of—anyone?'

Somehow it was too hard to mention her grandmother by name, but James was shaking his head anyway. 'Not in the immediate vicinity,' he denied, 'but they're probably searching for us, just as we're searching for them.'

'Take me there!' She looked at him as she never had before, her eyes huge and appealing, not looking at, but stunningly conscious of, the broad tanned torso that was glossy with the heat and vulnerably naked because she was wearing his shirt. 'Please, James!'

He held her gaze for a moment, and little fluttering sensations flitted up and down her spine. Then he nodded, turning as he did so and taking her arm, drawing her along with him and taking no account of her shorter stride; a fact she did not complain of in this instance. It was, as he had said, about twenty-five yards, but in that kind of terrain it seemed so much farther, and Rowan was panting breathlessly when he pointed out something sleek and smooth and half hidden among the rampant undergrowth.

In silence she left his side and hurried forward, staring down and only half believing, at the little boat leaning drunkenly against a tree with its side stove in. It was empty, but whereas she saw little significance in that, James realised the significance, and took heart from it obviously. 'They've taken everything with them,' he remarked, and went on to explain when Rowan looked at him hopefully. 'It was, of course, equipped with rations and a first aid box,' he pointed out, 'and both have gone. The rugs we snatched out of the deckchairs could have gone overboard, but not the things that were in the locker. I gave Paul the log too and that was in there.'

'But how do you know they haven't gone overboard too?' Rowan ventured, because she dared not be too optimistic, and James was shaking his head.

'The locker's under the centreboard, as you can see; when I found it it was closed but empty, which suggests to me that the act of closing it was a reflex action on some-one's part. Probably Maggie's, it's the kind of thing a woman would do automatically.'

For the first time Rowan allowed herself to believe it and she swallowed hard, her eyes shimmering in the green light under the trees. 'Then—you really believe she's—they're all right?'

'It looks very much like it,' James concurred, and his smile did so much to cheer her that she was filled with a wild excitement suddenly.

'Oh, James, just think——' Her laugh had a light shivery sound, and she reached up impulsively to put her arms around his neck, her mouth warm and light when she kissed him. 'Thank you, James!'

Rowan expected he would smile, but instead he looked at her with an expression that set her blood pounding. Both hands clasped her round her waist, sliding up under his shirt, his long hard fingers pressing into her yielding flesh and drawing her closer until the hard virility of his body pulsed its demands through the few clothes she wore, teasing her senses in a way that both excited and alarmed her. His breath on her lips was warm and slightly uneven until his mouth plunged deeply and suddenly, and took hers with an almost savage force.

It seemed to go on for ever, then, breathless and unable to think very clearly, Rowan rested her forehead on his chest while he pressed a light, brief and surprisingly dispassionate kiss on the nape of her neck. 'You're a wee smasher,' James murmured against her ear, 'but you make me forget what has to be done!' The timbre of his voice suggested he was smiling, and he lightly kissed her neck again before easing her away from him. 'Nor do I want to come to blows with René over you at the moment,' he went on, and shook his head over an attempted objection. 'So forget I did that, hmm?'

'Of course!'

If there was bitterness in her reply, she could not help it, for in her natural habitat Rowan was not accustomed to having men dismiss her kisses so lightly. Nor did she relish his assumption that René's claim to her was a valid one. Had it not been for that small abandoned boat lying there among the trees she might have pursued the matter of René, but there were other and more important things to concern her at the moment, and James seemed almost relieved when she changed the subject.

'Is there any sign of them—Grand'mère and the others, having gone on from here?' she asked, and James pointed out similar signs to those that had enabled her to follow him through the trees.

'See for yourself,' he said. 'Vines broken and branches snapped; the same kind of trail we left yesterday.'

His confidence encouraged her further, and she was more wildly excited at the prospect of finding her grandmother, though in this instance she refrained from expressing herself quite so uninhibitedly. Instead she suggested what she thought was the obvious thing to do in the circumstances, bubbling with enthusiasm, and impatient to do something practical.

'Let's go and find them!' she said, and would have darted past James had he not put a restraining hand on her arm. There was, she noticed, a curiously wry smile on his lips.

'Don't you think we'd better let René know first?' he suggested quietly, and Rowan brought herself swiftly back to earth.

'Oh yes, of course,' she murmured. 'I didn't think.'

She looked up again quickly when a long finger was laid over her lips. 'Let's go and tell him, shall we?' said James. But she noticed he did not take her hand or even her arm, only walked close enough to keep her aware of the virile strength of him so that she brushed a finger lightly and quite unconsciously across her mouth.

René was awake when they got back, and inevitably he scowled his dislike at seeing them together while he blinked the sleep from his eyes. He would almost certainly have remarked on their being together while he slept, but Rowan forestalled him by gabbling out the news James had brought them. Her hands clasped tightly together and her eyes bright with a desperate optimism, she spoke quickly and a little breathlessly.

'René, what do you think? James has found the boat; the dinghy from the *Belle*— it's out there among the trees! Isn't it marvellous? I can hardly believe we've actually got a clue at last; I'm so excited I could——'

She caught James' eye at that point and hastily looked away again when one light brow flicked upward briefly. René could have been more enthusiastic, she thought, but perhaps he was still dazed with sleep for he obviously hadn't been awake very long. He got to his feet, easing his cramped muscles and barely suppressing a yawn, then he placed an arm around Rowan's shoulders and drew her into the curve of his arm, bending to kiss her mouth.

'I'm so pleased, *chérie*,' he murmured, making a point

of speaking close to her ear so that James could scarcely
have heard what he said. 'I know how worried you were
about your *grand'mère* and how unhappy you've been because of it.' Again his mouth sought hers, insistent and
possessive, heedless of James' heavy-lidded gaze on them.
'Oh, my sweet Rowan, it's so good to see you smile again!'

She hesitated to draw away from him too pointedly, but
in fact she wasn't happy about that air of possessiveness,
though she could not have said exactly why. René professed
to love her, and since James had let it be known that he had
no claim in that direction, there was no reason for him not
to make a show of his feelings for fear of causing further
dissension. But still she was uneasy about it.

In fact she contrived eventually to slip out of his embrace
by bending to run an easing finger round the inside of one
of her uncomfortable shoes. When she straightened up
again she had managed to move out of reach and she
wondered if either he or James had noticed the manoeuvre.
'We're going to look for them right away,' she told René,
and laughed a little unsteadily when he gave James an
enquiring look. 'We'll just have to find our own breakfasts
this morning, as we go along. We can't afford to waste
any time.'

Whether or not James was in sympathy with the idea,
René looked vaguely dubious, and once again his brief
glance seemed to consult James' opinion. 'Do we know
where to look?' he asked, and obviously was not expecting
a very encouraging answer, from his expression.

'They've left a trail through the undergrowth just like
we did on our way here,' Rowan told him, slipping in
quickly before James had the opportunity to answer.
'James noticed it, and if we follow it we're bound to come
on them sooner or later. That's right, isn't it, James?'

His confirmation was a slightly paternal smile and a nod,
and he ran both hands through his uncombed hair until it
stood out like a mane; coarse and tawny gold, like the

Leo man Grand'mère had called him. 'I think we've a pretty good chance,' he agreed, then looked at René for a moment with an air of speculation. 'Do you feel up to it yet, René?'

'Why shouldn't I?' René demanded. Prickly as a hedge-hog, thought Rowan, and sighed inwardly at the prospect of further clashes between the two men who, only hours ago, had been such close friends.

With admirable restraint James sought to explain, but there was a rough edge on the soft rolling tones that Rowan noticed, whether or not René did. 'You've quite a bruise on your chin where you hit when you went overboard last night,' he pointed out, 'and it's quite plain you're not fully awake. I'm merely suggesting that if you *don't* feel like making tracks right away as Rowan's proposing to do, you let me go on ahead while the two of you stay on here for a bit.'

René had the grace to look a little sheepish, but he still thrust out his lower lip in that petulant, reproachful way, as if he alone was having to endure the present hardships. Then he reached and placed his arm around Rowan again, looking at her for a moment before he said anything. 'I can see the sense in that,' he allowed, 'but would Rowan stay with me?'

It was a choice she hated having to make, and Rowan's heart was thudding anxiously when she looked across at James, seeking his guidance as usual, but finding it hard to believe he was set on leaving her behind in this instance. He must know how anxious she was to go, and more especially since it seemed possible he would find the rest of their party. Yet René, on the other hand, obviously pre-ferred to stay and seemed to need her so much that she found it hard to refuse him.

James' heavy lids concealed his eyes and he gave her no help, but René eyed her anxiously. 'If you want to stay——' she began, but with such obvious reluctance that René shook his head and silenced her.

'Oh no, I should have thought!' He tightened his arm around her, pulling her close. 'I know how anxious you are to find your *grand'mère*, and if they aren't far away——' Shaking his head slowly, he rubbed the back of his free hand across a forehead already beaded with perspiration. 'Of course we'll go and find them, *chérie*, it's what you want to do, and you're right.' He bent and kissed her mouth, a moist lingering kiss that Rowan would have avoided if she could. 'I'm sorry, Rowan; I'm a selfish devil, I know, but this damned place brings out the worst in me.' The smile he gave her showed traces of the confidence and charm she remembered from what seemed like a lifetime ago, and his blue eyes moved slowly and searchingly over her features, as if even the promise of a reunion with the rest of their party was enough to boost his flagging self-confidence. 'When we get back to civilisation, *chérie*, I'll more than make up to you for all this!'

His meaning was in no doubt, and again Rowan was made conscious of James standing by, not forgotten but silent for the moment and apparently detached from them mentally if not physically. For some reason she did not altogether understand, Rowan wished she knew what was going on in his mind.

René's words reminded her of something else too; the fact that finding her grandmother and the rest of their party was only part of their problem. There was also the matter of how they were to get back to what René referred to as civilisation, and that could well prove to be the hardest part of all; she dared not think yet of the possibility of their not getting back. That train of thought, though, made it instinctive to glance at James where he stood slightly apart and oddly detached, because she once more needed the hope and optimism that only he could give her.

She thought he met her eyes but couldn't be sure, and he was already half-turned when he spoke, as if he was impatient to be away. 'If you've made up your minds, let's get going, shall we?' he said.

He plunged immediately into the mass of undergrowth and Rowan and René followed him without question, René's arm around her shoulders for as long as it was practicable. Only now, Rowan felt, the embrace was as much a sign of his need for support as of possessiveness.

Even though a path had already been cut through for them, the going was still hard, and they had long since passed the spot where the abandoned lifeboat leaned drunkenly among the trees, with so far no sign of its former occupants. As they were following an already beaten track, René apparently saw no reason for him to go ahead with James, and he stayed in the rear with Rowan, holding her hand tightly, and cursing more and more as the way stretched on.

It became more unbearably hot as the sun rose higher, and Rowan told herself she would give anything for a bath. Even that ice-cold spring water they had bathed in yesterday would have been welcome; but better still would be a shower with endless supplies of bath essence and soap and a huge soft towel to dry herself on.

She was snatched rudely from her daydream when René went sprawling on the ground in front of her suddenly, and lay there unmoving, ominously limp and silent.

'James!' she shouted.

It was instinct that made her call to him, and James turned at once. He came back and dropped to one knee beside René, but drew back hastily when René turned over and sat up, cursing volubly in French and glaring at them both in turn. Neither Rowan nor James said a word for several seconds, but a flock of birds took off from the trees overhead, screeching frenzidly, as if the violence of his reaction startled them rather than the sounds he made.

'I turned my damned ankle, that's all!' René complained

harshly, and glared at the offending limb in despair. 'Why me?' he went on, stressing his grievance with a rolled fist on his forehead and gritting his teeth. 'Of all the stupid, clumsy damned——'

'Cussing isn't going to do much to help,' James broke in quietly, 'but if it makes you feel any better, go ahead. I don't suppose Rowan minds in the circumstances.'

'In the circumstances!' René muttered between tight lips. 'I shouldn't have made such a fool of myself in civilised circumstances!'

'For God's sake, man,' James told him, 'stop feeling sorry for yourself and let me take a look at your ankle!'

'You——'

'Oh, stop it, both of you!'

Rowan cut him short, her own discomfort and tiredness showing in the higher, more shrill pitch of her voice, and both men turned and looked up at her for a moment. René looked not only surprised but reproachful, while James, after a moment or two speculating, smiled faintly and nodded his head.

'You're right, Rowan,' he allowed, 'losing our tempers with each other isn't going to help.'

Vaguely embarrassed by his approval, Rowan knelt hastily on the other side of René and rolled back the bottom of his trouser leg to look at the injury. It was already swollen and it looked painful, but when she tested its movement it proved not to be broken, which was one thing to be grateful for. Nevertheless it wouldn't help their progress over the kind of terrain they were coping with, and she foresaw more delay.

'It hurts like hell!' René stated unhelpfully, and just for a moment Rowan felt an hysterical and almost irresistible desire to giggle at his determined self-pity. René, deprived of his comfortable and sophisticated background, had rapidly lost much of his smooth charm and confidence. 'How am I going to get on now, with a broken ankle to contend with?' he demanded, and James shook his head.

'Not broken, sprained,' he corrected him mildly, and grimaced in sympathy. 'It's going to hurt when you walk on it, but——'

'Walk!'

René looked appalled at the idea, but it was clear that James saw no alternative, and once more Rowan took note of the tiredness etched in tiny lines around his mouth and eyes. 'I can't carry you, man,' he said quietly. 'Over this kind of ground it just isn't feasible, I'd be likely to fall and break *my* leg, and I can't see poor wee Rowan lugging both of us back to civilisation, can you?'

René's dark eyes had a blank, helpless look that it was hard not to sympathise with, for all his self-pity; and she had no reason to believe that James felt any less for him than she did herself. If the only alternative was for René to wait behind, she guessed he would manage somehow, but he was finding it all too much to cope with. And whereas aboard the yacht the few years' difference in age between him and James had been scarcely noticeable, René now seemed so much more immature in comparison, so much less able to face the situation they found themselves in.

'As far as possible,' James told him in his quietly confident voice, 'we'll walk abreast and you can hang on to me. I'll support you as best I can, but through the awkward bits you'll mebbe have to scrabble along as best you can.'

'You can lean on me too,' said Rowan, and met the look in James' icy-blue eyes challengingly. 'I can take some of the weight, I'm not helpless, you know, and you can't take on everything, James. You're as bone-weary as the rest of us.'

How he could smile she would never know, but he showed his strong teeth briefly between parched lips, and shook his head. 'You *are* a wee smasher,' he murmured, ignoring René's inevitable frown. He bent to help René to his feet, Rene's arm across his broad shoulders as he heaved him up on to what looked suspiciously like a deserted anthill, then stood looking down at him with an expression of mingled sympathy and exasperation. 'Now I'll have to deprive you of *your* shirt, unless you've anything else will do to bind your ankle,' he told him. 'Mebbe if we take out the sleeves it will do.'

René eventually shrugged and parted with his damp and dirty shirt while they tore the sleeves out of it, but when he resumed what was left of it his face showed quite clearly how much he disliked looking so ragged and unkempt. The sleeves alone provided enough material to make a firm support for the injured foot, and Rowan watched, fascinated, while James used the makeshift bandage neatly and efficiently, having refused her offer of assistance.

'Jack of all trades?' she suggested softly, and he glanced up at her over his shoulder.

'Even master of some,' he challenged, and she smiled, unable to deny it.

Getting him on to his feet was the next problem, and Rowan took a hand there because she felt she might have more influence than James. 'Try standing,' she urged. 'Lean on James and me and see how it feels.'

'It hurts!'

'Of course it does!' She hastily subdued her impatience. 'But try it!'

He eventually put an arm around her shoulders only, ignoring James, and tentatively put his foot to the ground, and it could have been the unconscious look of warning in her eyes that decided his verdict. 'If you'll just give me a minute or two, I can manage,' he said, then seemed to notice James with his hands on his hips, watching him. Despite his tiredness, his tanned and gleaming body gave him a strongly primitive air that Rowan found infinitely disturbing, but annoyed René because it seemed to stress his own helplessness. 'Glare all you like, we need a breather anyway,' he insisted, obviously anticipating an argument, and the way he looked at Rowan put the onus firmly on to her.

'I hate to stop now we're slowed down still more,' she told him, and her eyes were wide and appealing, 'but I suppose we do all need a few minutes, James.'

He looked at her for a long moment in silence and her heavy heart had a curiously uneven beat to it suddenly that beat like a drum in her head. Then he nodded and half-smiled. 'You're dead beat, aren't you, girl?' he guessed softly, and she barely moved her head to acknowledge it. 'Then sit down for just a wee while and rest.'

He lowered his own long length on to the damp ground too, and from the way he moved it was clear that even his healthy physique was being tried to the point of defeat. Rowan knew she had never in her life felt more tired and hopeless, and the optimism of early morning had been reduced by the last two hours' long trek. Looking across at him, she tried not to show how her faith had dwindled, but it was hard to do.

'They—it can't be much further now, can it, James?' she asked. 'I mean they can't have gone very far, can they?'

He was shaking his head, but she thought it was more to discourage a wild guess and possible disappointment rather than to deny a rapid end to their quest. 'I wish I knew,' he told her, then smiled in the way that always lifted her spirits. 'But we're obviously on the right track because someone's broken the trail for us, and with the *Belle*'s lifeboat as a clue I don't see how we can be following anyone but Maggie and her merry men, do you?'

'It *must* be!' Rowan sat with her knees drawn up tight and her hands pressed to her mouth, her eyes showing a haze of despair that she did her best to conceal. 'I don't think——' She coped with a choking lump in her throat suddenly, and pressed her hands so tightly to her quivering lips that the knuckles bruised her flesh. Bending to rest her forehead on her knees, she let the silky limp mass of her hair drift forward and hide her face. 'It isn't worth all this otherwise,' she murmured in a muffled voice. 'It simply isn't worth it!'

'Rowan!'

James' deep quiet voice with its rolling r reached her in soft warning, but as if he anticipated a more physical contact, René slid down from his elevated mound and on to the ground beside her. More than once since their dramatic arrival on the island he had stood by and seen James comfort her, and he meant to forestall him this time. Putting his arms around her shoulders, he held her close, smoothing one hand over her hair.

'Darling, it's all right, don't worry. It'll be all right, you'll see.'

But to Rowan there was a vast difference in the feeling it gave her, being in his arms and in James', yet she could not have said exactly why. René held her close, just as James had, and soothed her with a hand over her hair, murmuring in her ear and hugging her tight. But the heartbeat that throbbed under her cheek had the rapid and unmistakable urgency of despair, unlike the steady, strong beat of James', and with René she got the feeling that she was comforting as much as being comforted.

'We'll make it, *chérie*,' he whispered, but Rowan was sure that as he said it he looked across at James for confirmation.

It was James' voice a second or so later that made her lift her head and look at him in obvious dismay. 'We'll make it quicker mebbe if I go on while you two take a breather,' he said, and Rowan noticed how he avoided her eyes suddenly. 'I'll not lose you if I keep on the way we're going, and I'll come back for you, I promise.' His smile had a tight and not quite genuine look about it, but it was reassuring just the same. 'I might even bring Maggie back with me to take care of our casualty!'

He stood toweringly tall over them, and never in her life had Rowan been so afraid of being left, though she tried hard to conceal it since he seemed set on going alone. 'You —you think you might find them?' she asked huskily, and he met her eyes for a moment, their ice blue warm and gentle.

'I've a feeling, girl,' he told her softly, 'but don't bet your shirt on it.' His gaze slid down to his grubby towelling shirt, low enough in the neck to show the soft swell of her breasts, and he smiled. 'My shirt, I should say,' he added, then bent swiftly and kissed the top of her head. 'I'll try not to be too long, and for God's sake don't try to follow me—wait! O.K.?'

Rowan nodded. 'We'll wait,' she promised, while René merely nodded without speaking. Rowan watched him, all too soon half concealed among the unfriendly undergrowth, and briefly her heart tripped in panic so that she called after him without really realising her own intent. 'James!' He turned and looked back at her, only just stopping himself from running back, she thought. 'Don't go—I mean—be careful!'

She sensed René's frown, but James raised a hand after a second, in a casual salute. 'See you!' he promised, and was out of sight all too soon.

CHAPTER FIVE

IT was not much more than an hour since James had left them. Rowan knew because although her own wristwatch had been damaged by the sea water, René's was still functioning and she had checked the time on several occasions during the past sixty minutes or so. It was hard to believe how much more nervous she felt because she and René were on their own. Every little movement in the tree tops or among the thick undergrowth that hemmed in the clearing set her heart thudding anxiously, and her eyes darted swiftly and instinctively to the spot where she had seen James last. She dared not allow herself to speculate on what might happen if he did not come back as he had promised.

René on the other hand seemed to be fairly relaxed at the moment. At least he was not complaining; in fact it was clear that he saw advantages to James being absent. Too restless to settle in any one place, Rowan had initially roamed around the small clearing until yielding eventually to René's pleas to sit down. Then choosing a spot some distance from where he sat, she hugged her knees, listening all the time for sounds of James returning, while she talked about the prospect of his finding the others. Never once had she given any indication of the gnawing fear deep inside her that they never would find them; keeping up her own morale and, she hoped, René's too.

Eventually he had coaxed her closer so that he could lay an arm around her shoulders while the fingers of his hand rested lightly on the curve that swelled softly beneath the over-sized shirt she was wearing. Turning his head, he lightly kissed the lobe of her ear, then blew warmly on her neck, sending little trickles of sensation fluttering over her skin that weren't at all unpleasant.

She had no intention of letting René know that her head ached or that she occasionally felt a twinge of nausea. There was no point in worrying him and it was probably nothing more than the effect of the heat. She had never been in the tropics before, and she had been forced to indulge in some pretty strenuous exercise during the past couple of days. At least she had stopped perspiring so much, she noticed, although her skin felt burningly hot and dry, which was hardly more comfortable.

Sitting beside René, she stretched out her legs in front of her and leaned her head back against his arm, closing

her eyes against the sun that tipped over the tops of the
trees into the tiny clearing that was scarcely a clearing at
all. She had never felt so limp and bone-weary in her life
before, she was sure of it, and there would be more trek-
king to do when James came back for them. It was inevitable whether or not he found her grandmother and the
rest of the crew.

'O.K.?' René asked, and when he leaned over and kissed
her mouth she opened her eyes for a second.

'I'm fine.'

'No regrets?' She opened her eyes and frowned up at
him curiously. 'You're not sorry you stayed with me instead of going off with James?' René added, and Rowan's
smile was so faint it scarcely touched her lips and never
reached her eyes.

'I'm not sure I had the energy to go with him anyway,'
she told him, evasive rather than untruthful.

'Well, I'm grateful to have you to myself for a while,'
René murmured. 'I've never really been alone with you,
chérie, do you realise that? Never—not quite alone as we
are now.'

'No, I suppose not.'

Her reply was not deliberately offhand, but she realised
the moment she spoke that it sounded so and that René
would take her up on it. It was simply that she found it
difficult to detach her mind from the fact of their complete isolation. They had surely had their share of crises
already, but if anything did happen while James was away
she hadn't much faith in either her own or René's ability
to deal with it. René was virtually immobile and she had
proved herself to be a complete innocent abroad without
James' help.

She was increasingly anxious about his absence and more
nervous than she cared to admit. No doubt in normal circumstances she would have scoffed at the idea of being
so dependent on any man, but at the moment all she knew

was that until James came back she couldn't give her mind to anything or anyone else.

'Rowan? *Mignonne?*' As she expected, her unresponsive mood irritated René, although he disguised it with a smile for the moment, studying her with an archness that seemed uncomfortably out of place in the circumstances. 'Aren't you glad we have some time to ourselves?' Cupping a hand to her cheek, he turned her face, and when he kissed her his eyes were as dark and glowingly ardent as they had been that evening on the deck of the yacht. 'Oh, Rowan, I love you so much, and I want to marry you, *ma belle*. I want to marry you; doesn't that touch you at all?'

To Rowan it was neither the time nor the place, and she stirred uneasily in his encircling arm. He was in earnest, she had no doubt, but whatever response he could have hoped for in normal circumstances, at the moment she was able to give such matters no more than a passing thought. Very firmly, she moved away from the too intimate caress of the hand over her shoulder, then shook her head.

'I'm very touched, René,' she told him. 'I—I appreciate that it's something very special when a man asks you to marry him——'

'*But!*' René guessed harshly.

Rowan bit anxiously into her lower lip, unprepared for this particular contingency and mindful of making matters worse if she said the wrong thing. 'I'm not unfeeling, René, or unappreciative, but I thought I'd made it clear how I felt. I tried to explain that last night on board the *Belle*, I just don't want to be committed to anything yet. I—I don't know my own mind and I don't think I can think about it seriously enough at this moment and in this situation.'

René's lip was pursed in that increasingly familiar expression of petulance, and he eyed her suspiciously, noting her heat-flushed cheeks, and the restless eyes that again and again strayed, as if compelled, to the edge of the encroaching jungle. 'And I suppose you still say it has nothing to do with James?'

Rowan frowned at him curiously. She was completely at a loss until she recalled that once before, what seemed like a lifetime ago, she had been asked that same question. She had insisted then that James Fraser had nothing whatever to do with her decision, and on that occasion it had been easy to sound convincing because she believed it herself. But since then she had become so dependent on James for so many things that she spoke with much less conviction.

'Of course it has nothing to do with James!'

'I find that very hard to believe in view of recent events!' René accused harshly. 'It seems to me that he's made a lot of progress, too much for my liking, since this damned nightmare started; and you've scarcely taken your eyes of the place where he—disappeared! Just how *do* you feel about him, Rowan?'

Rowan's silence was perhaps a fraction too long, but she was unwilling to admit what her feelings were where James was concerned. She was not even sure she knew for certain herself. 'I'm depending on him to find Grand'mère and to get us away from here, that's all!' Her voice shivered uncertainly, and almost before the words were out of her mouth she regretted the calculating and impersonal nature of them. 'No! No, that isn't all.' She hastened to make amends. 'I owe James my life, for one thing, and I'm eternally grateful for all he's done since we landed here. He's been so kind and—and understanding, and he——'

'He's bullied us both, unmercifully!' René protested.

'Only because he had to!' Her protest was as impassioned as his, and she realised too late that it wasn't the kind of answer that René wanted to hear.

He turned her to face him again and his fingers pressed

almost bruisingly hard into her cheek, the dark gleam of resentment in his eyes. 'You've fallen for that strong-arm routine of his!' he accused, and despite his vehemence it was possible to detect a plaintive note. René, she realised, was not accustomed to being denied what he wanted, and she wondered vaguely why she had never realised before that jealousy lurked below that friendly relationship he had with James. 'He *has* taken you from me, no matter how much he denies it!' he insisted, and Rowan sighed in despair.

Her head was throbbing like a drum and she hadn't the least desire to argue the point, although it was fairly obvious she wasn't going to be given an option. 'That's nonsense, René, and I wish you wouldn't keep harping on the same thing again and again! Let it rest—please!'

But she might as well not have spoken, she realised when he continued in the same vein still. 'He's never cheated me with a woman before; why in God's name did it have to be *you*?'

'Oh, for heaven's sake, René!'

She shrugged away from him, uneasy because she could so clearly remember every second she had been in James' arms that morning, and the hard, erotic touch of his mouth, the hands that had roused such wild emotions in her that she scarcely recognised herself. Shaking off the recollection, she shook her head determinedly.

'How can I make you understand?' she asked in desperation. 'I'm not—in love with anyone; I'm not even thinking about being in love, with James or you, or anyone else! What must I do to convince you?'

'But, *chérie*, you must know——'

'*No!*' Her insistence silenced him, but his hands betrayed how dissatisfied he was with the situation, and the agitated movement of his fingers did more to win her sympathy than all his words had. 'René—I'm sorry, truly I am, but I just can't think about anything at the moment except

finding Grand'mère and getting home again. I thought you
realised and understood that.'

'I do.'

The admission was made reluctantly, she suspected, and
Rowan gave him a very small and uncertain smile. 'I'm
just not thinking very straight about anything at the moment,' she confessed. 'I just feel—limp.'

In fact she felt overwhelmed suddenly by tiredness and
anxiety and sheer physical discomfort. She did not want
to cry, but she seemed incapable of doing anything about
it, and through the tears that momentarily blinded her, she
glanced yet again across the clearing. For all her denials, she
would have given anything to have James there at that moment; calm, soothing and understanding; a shoulder to
cry on.

In fact it was René who reached out suddenly and
gathered her into his arms, murmuring softly against her
ear; anxious and apologetic. 'Oh, Rowan, I'm sorry, my
darling, I'm such a thoughtless brute! I don't know how
I could have been so blind—forgive me, *ma chère*!'
Rowan clung to him because at that moment he was the
only other human being in that small and cruelly hostile
world, and he patted and soothed her anxiously. 'Oh, my
sweet darling Rowan, don't cry, please don't cry!'

It was a relief to be close to him, to anyone, and to hide
from the sight of the endless venue of tangled trees and
vines, and of cloying, sticky marsh that steamed obscenely
in the heat. Then slowly she raised her head from René's
shoulder and the moment she did he bent and pressed his
lips firmly to hers, stifling what she had been going to say.
The move was so adroitly quick and unheralded that for
a moment she did nothing, only yielded instinctively, subduing her wretchedness in the undeniable pleasure of his
kiss.

Her heavy lids were already fluttering open when she
caught sight of a movement from the corner of her eye

and turned her head quickly. She broke free of René's embrace, ignoring his protest, and scrambled to her feet, shaking like a leaf at the sight of the tall and disturbingly primitive figure standing just where the trees edged the clearing.

'James!'

He stood motionless, as if the sight of René kissing her had brought him up short, and Rowan's heart was thudding hard as she waited for him to move closer. She did not understand his immobility, and her first thought was that he had failed, for there was a dark look in his eyes that suggested defeat rather than triumph, and a tight look about his mouth. Then he moved across the clearing towards them, his lean body taut with some emotion that gave him the menacing prowl of a big cat.

'Is—are you all right?' He looked faintly surprised at the query, and she hurried on, breathless and excited despite her anxiety. 'Did you find them—anyone?'

'I found them,' said James, and she clasped her hands together, pressing them to her lips for a moment while her eyes beamed anxiously above her praying fingers.

There was a small flutter of doubt nagging away at the back of her mind; a suspicion that she dared not acknowledge. 'Are they—are they far away?' Of course they couldn't be far away because he had been gone not much over an hour. 'It can't be far,' she went on without waiting for confirmation. 'Oh, James, if she—is Grand'mère O.K.?'

'Did I not promise she'd be fighting fit?' James asked. His smile beamed at her briefly, but by now Rowan was so familiar with every feature of him that she noticed it did not show in his eyes. 'As you said, it isn't very far from here, and as soon as we can get René up on his feet I'll take you there.'

'Oh, James!'

She said it softly and almost like a prayer, for whatever

the circumstances, she believed she would never have found her grandmother again without him. Again, as she had earlier that day, she felt an almost irresistible urge to throw her arms around his neck and kiss him; only in this instance she resisted because she knew René would more than likely spoil the whole wonderful moment if she did.

As it was she shook her head slowly from side to side, letting her wide grey eyes express how she felt, shimmering and glowing between long lashes as she looked at him. It was because she looked at him so intently that it dawned on her there was something more than he had told them, and she regarded him for a moment with her head tilted to one side. 'James? What—what is it?' she asked softly.

James ran a hand through his mane of hair before he answered, and she could almost feel the tension in him, her own senses tingling and wary. 'Your grannie and Paul Ordin are O.K.,' he told her in an obviously controlled voice that made his sudden violence even more startling, 'but Bill and poor old Steven were lost in that—that damned storm!'

His vehemence came as a shock, but Rowan knew how he must be feeling. All his crew had been with him for a number of years, and they were more than simply people who worked for him. 'Oh, James, I'm so sorry, I——' Her voice trembled uncertainly, then broke off, and she spread her hands in a gesture of helplessness. Her head throbbed like a drum and burned as if it was on fire, but all she could think of was how James must be feeling, and she was assailed by a need to comfort him as he had so often comforted her during the past couple of days. 'I don't know what to say,' she whispered.

James' pale eyes warmed for a moment, and he reached out and stroked his long fingers down her cheek. 'There's nothing you *can* say, girl,' he told her softly, and laid his finger-tips lightly on the pulse in her neck. Then he frowned as if he had discovered something else that disturbed him; placing a hand on her forehead and watching her face as he did so. 'Are you all right?' he asked, and there was a hard edge on his voice.

'I'm fine!' She answered him as she had René earlier, backing away from his hand. Not because she found his touch repellant to her, on the contrary, it was light and soothing and eased her throbbing head, but because she did not want him to suspect she was not perfectly well either. 'I'm tough, don't you realise that yet?'

'I know you've not said a word of complaint since we started on this blasted safari,' James replied bluntly. 'That's not quite the same thing! You're on fire, and I don't like it—come here!'

The instruction took her by surprise and Rowan backed still further away, her eyes bright and wary, evading the big hands that reached out for her. 'I'm all right, James, honestly.'

'You're a rotten liar!' James retorted, and ignored René's indignant protest as if he wasn't there. 'Come here and let me take a look at you, Rowan. Oh, for God's sake, I'll not hurt you!' he declared in exasperation. 'Don't be daft, girl, just come here where I can look at you!'

'I'm all *right*!' Rowan insisted, then gasped when he reached out and pulled her towards him, his hands sliding up under the towelling shirt and feeling her hot dry skin with his hard fingers, under her arms and her breasts and in the small of her back, a curiously firm but impersonal touch to which she submitted without protest, limp and still.

'*Damn* you!' René glared at him fiercely, trying to get up from his immobilising seat on the ground, but James paid him no heed. 'Damn you, James!'

'You're as dry as a bone.' James pronounced his verdict and somehow managed to make it sound accusing. 'What else is wrong, Rowan? Do you feel dizzy or sick?'

'No, no, no, no!'

'For God's sake,' René objected, scowling fiercely in frustration because it was harder than he realised to get up from the ground with one ankle out of action. 'What's the matter with you? Hasn't Rowan said she's all right? Since when were you a doctor of medicine anyway?'

'I'm a doctor of experience!' James informed him shortly, but kept his eyes on Rowan while he spoke. 'I've spent long enough in this kind of climate to know something of the nasties it can come up with, and I've a suspicion Rowan isn't telling me the truth; are you?'

'I *am* all right, James.' Her voice sounded very small and unsteady and she wished she had more control over it. 'Please—can't we go on? I'm not ill, I promise you, I'm perfectly all right.'

Heaven knew what option he had, but Rowan heaved an inward sigh of relief when, after studying her for a moment or two, James nodded. 'I can't see an alternative at the moment,' he confessed, 'but the minute we get there you're for the treatment, my girl, take my word for it!' His mouth relaxed just briefly and that curiously wry half-smile touched its corners. 'Let's go and find Maggie, shall we?' he said softly.

Feeling himself ignored and resenting the attention she was getting from James, René hit out, unthinking, as he so often was. 'And where are we going?' he demanded harshly. 'To yet another clearing in this blasted swamp, I suppose! Oh, believe me, I've just about *had* mud and trees up to here!'

He made a short chopping gesture towards his own throat, and James stood looking down at him for a moment, saying nothing, though Rowan could sense the anger that he kept so firmly under control. His eyes had the gleam of silvery steel between their pale lashes, and for the first time since the whole wretched business began, she believed he was close to losing his temper.

'For God's sake, man, be thankful you're alive!' he told

him. 'Others weren't so lucky!'

It was only when René frowned at him blankly that Rowan realised James had spoken too quietly for him to have heard about the two crew members, and she hastened to enlighten him before James went on to say something she could believe he would be sorry for. 'It's Bill and old Steven,' she told him in a small voice. 'They—they were lost in the storm, René.'

It came as a shock, that was clear, although nothing that did not directly concern René would affect him very deeply, she suspected. 'I'm sorry,' he said, and might tactfully have left the matter there. But the sight of James' brief but searching examination of Rowan was too clear in his mind and it pushed him beyond the bounds of reason. 'But that doesn't excuse the way you were going on with Rowan just now,' he insisted, and Rowan drew a long shuddering breath of exasperation.

James held tight to his temper, but his voice was deep and harsh when he answered him, making it clear that he spoke the truth. 'For your information,' he told him, 'Rowan is going to be very, very ill if she goes on as she is, and my main concern now is to get her somewhere where she can be treated quickly.'

Quite obviously René was stunned, and he stared up at him blankly. 'How—how do you know?' he pressed, and James ran an impatient hand through his hair as he shook his head.

'Because I know something about tropical climates and the kind of effect it can have on people not accustomed to it.'

Rowan was in two minds just how serious he was. She felt increasingly as though her whole body was on fire and her head ached abominably, but the circumstances could account for that. And maybe James was simply trying to impress René with the fact that there were others to consider apart from himself.

'Darling.' René looked up at her, and Rowan saw the darkness of apprehension in his blue eyes as she clasped his hand automatically. 'I didn't realise you were ill,' he said. 'I'd no idea you were——'

'I'm not ill, René.' She gave James a brief reproachful look before she denied it, and pressed René's hand reassuringly. 'I'm perfectly O.K., and I promise you I'll make it to wherever Grand'mère is, if I have to crawl there on all fours!'

'You're sure?' He was probably so easily convinced because he wanted to be, Rowan thought; and she really had no more than a headache and occasional nausea, very likely brought on by their unconventional diet.

'I'm quite sure,' she insisted.

Almost certainly James was regretting his outburst, for he was, Rowan would have sworn, not a vindictive man. He stood for a moment looking down at René, then gave him a faintly rueful smile as he bent to help him to his feet. 'Come on, man,' he said, heaving upward with his powerful shoulders. 'Let's have you on your one good leg, and get the hell out of here!' He gave Rowan a warning frown when she stepped forward to share some of the burden on her own shoulders, and shook his head. 'Not you,' he told her shortly. 'You need to conserve your strength if you're to make it to your grannie; just follow on behind.'

'But I can manage——'

'You can just do as you're damned well told!' James declared with a flash of temper. 'Let's have a little co-operation without argument for a change, for God's sake!' Perhaps it was her silent submission that got to him, obviously something did, for after a few moments he sent her a brief and slightly rueful grin over his shoulder that she could not help responding to. 'Would you believe they found what appears to be an abandoned conservation survey hut?' he told her. 'With a few useful odds and ends lying about; including a radio, although it's *kaput* at the moment.'

'A radio? Honestly?' His smile mocked her slightly naïve reaction, but Rowan didn't care at the moment. Even René brightened visibly and the fact of losing two of their number receded momentarily before their own better prospects. 'It's hard to believe in a place like this; fantastic! Can it be mended?'

'Paul seems to think so,' James told her with a face that suggested he shared his steward's optimism. 'He was radio operator on the *Belle* as well as steward, you know.'

'I didn't know.' Rowan's heart seemed to beat with more urgency and little flutters of excitement caused her to shiver with anticipation as she caught James' eye again, and she laughed, a light breathless sound. 'You were right about finding Grand'mère,' she said, 'let's hope you're right about that too.'

It was a relief to realise that the tight closed look seemed to have gone from his face for the time being, and when she met his eyes they warmed her with their secret smile for a moment. Once more the two of them seemed drawn close by that curious rapport that never consciously excluded René, yet did so inevitably.

It took them another twenty-five gruelling minutes, during which James had to half-carry René over terrain that was hard going even without an injured man along, before they found what they were looking for. Rowan heard James murmur something under his breath, and a moment later they walked through into a wide clearing, bigger than any they had seen so far.

It was like another world, even though the same dank jungle surrounded it. Bright and sunny and with the sound of running water somewhere close by, it seemed like paradise to Rowan, and right in the centre of it rose a mound of blessedly dry ground on which stood the building James had spoken of.

It was neither chalet nor hut to Rowan's mind, but a kind of bungalow that was falling apart with neglect and could never have been very prepossessing. It had one small window and a balcony running across its width, and while Rowan stared in joyous anticipation at the first real human habitation they had seen in days, Marguerite de Clare walked out on to the balcony.

'Grand'mère!'

At the sight of the endearingly familiar figure, tall and still somehow elegant in a crumpled and brine-soaked dress, Rowan slipped away from the arm René stretched out to her and darted across the expanse of open ground. Her legs felt alarmingly weak and shaky, but the sheer joy of being able to do other than clamber and slip over trees and vine roots exhilarated her, as well as the sight of her grandmother standing with arms outstretched. It seemed like so much longer than two days since they had bade one another goodnight and gone to their respective cabins, and as Rowan hugged her close, she could do nothing about the tears that flowed down her grimy cheeks unchecked.

'Oh, Grand'mère, Grand'mère!'

The enfolding arms held her tightly, rocking her back and forth as they had when she was a child, and for once Rowan was heedless of the two men who came more slowly across the clearing. Then she raised her head and brushed the tears away with a finger so that she could see the face that she had sometimes doubted she would ever see again; a face devoid of its customary discreet make-up, and frankly ageing. Placing gentle hands either side of her face, Marguerite smiled as if the whole world was suddenly laid at her feet.

'Oh, you look such a *gamine* I'm ashamed of you,' she said softly. 'But I'm so, *so* glad to see you, my little one; I had thought I never would again.'

Flushed and slightly lightheaded, Rowan turned to look

at James as he half carried René up the two steps to the balcony, her eyes showing much more than she realised. 'You never *would* have seen me again if James Fraser wasn't such a shocking bully,' she told her grandmother, and laughed in sheer relief. 'To begin with he towed me along with him, in that terrible sea, can you imagine? Then when I was able to swim by myself he bullied and cursed me every inch of the way to this awful little island. Even now I don't know how he managed to get me here in those conditions!'

'Simply because you're a stubborn, mule-headed little brat who didn't want to drown,' James declared with uninhibited frankness. 'Hello again, Maggie; I brought her back to you, you see.'

Marguerite's dark eyes shimmered with unshed tears and she moved to where he stood supporting René still, on the narrow board balcony, ignoring René for the moment while she took James' strong, weather-brown face between her hands and kissed him full on his mouth. 'You're so like your father, *mon ami*,' she murmured, fighting hard to steady her voice. 'And I'll never be able to thank you enough.'

He was slightly embarrassed by her emotional gratitude, Rowan thought, but he was gratified too and he smiled into her grandmother's eyes in that bold, impudent way he knew she would appreciate. 'I've brought us a patient, Maggie.' His glance flicked briefly in Rowan's direction, but he said nothing about her at the moment. 'Just a sprained ankle, but we've been hauling the poor beggar along for the past half-hour and it must hurt like hell.'

'Oh, my poor René!' He had Marguerite's immediate sympathy. 'Come, we must put cold compresses on it, *mon cher*, that will ease it for you and get rid of the swelling.'

She kissed him on both cheeks, murmuring sympathy and endearments as she led the way into the ramshackle bungalow, and reaching for Rowan's hand before she did so, as if she feared to lose her again. René, Rowan thought, would be every bit as sorry for himself as Marguerite was for him, but he contented himself with looking woebegone rather than say anything for the moment.

The door led straight into a big shady room that was furnished after a fashion, although what furniture there was was old and dilapidated and inevitably mildewed, and a musty damp smell pervaded the whole place. But it was a roof over their heads and it stood on firm ground, and after the past two days, to Rowan it seemed like sheer bliss.

It boasted an ordinary wooden slat chair, and another similar one with an extending foot-rest attached; both had cushions that were in an advanced state of mouldy disintegration, and most uninviting. There was a small and very rickety table in the centre of the floor, and shelves ran the whole width of the room on one wall. It had only one window and that looked out on to the clearing they had just left. It was without glass; a woven grass curtain, rolled back and tied with string, doing service instead.

The jumble of equipment in the far corner of the room among the shadows was obviously the radio James had mentioned, and Paul Ordin, erstwhile steward and radio-operator from the *Belle o' Dunoon*, sat working at it. He looked up briefly when they came in, and Rowan was shocked by his haggard, drawn look and the look in his eyes that showed how deep the loss of his companions had hurt him. James gave him a brief salute, and he nodded, then returned to his task.

With René safely seated in the chair with the foot-rest, James straightened up and his gaze fell immediately on Rowan. Marguerite was on her knees beside René, making soothing noises over his injured ankle, and for the moment fully occupied. But when James moved across beside her, Rowan's heart set up a wild, urgent beat because she remembered his threat to render some kind of treatment the minute they arrived, and there was a firm resolute look in the ice-blue eyes that told her he had not forgotten.

'How are you feeling?' he asked, in a low quiet voice that her grandmother couldn't have heard, she noted thankfully.

'I'm all right, James, I told you——'

'I know what you told me,' James cut in impatiently. 'But believe me I'm not that easily fooled, Rowan, and I've seen heat-stroke before.'

'Is that all——'

'It has to be treated,' he insisted firmly, 'and don't tell me you haven't a headache, or you don't feel sick; you look awful!'

'*Thank* you!'

Ignoring her throbbing head, Rowan glared at him, but James as always was impervious to discouragement and he called out to her grandmother. 'Is there a bed of any kind in this palace of yours, Maggie?'

Marguerite glanced briefly at him over her shoulder, obviously seeing nothing serious in the question. 'Of a sort,' she told him, 'but it's no more than a bunk in an incredibly tiny room, and it would never take your long length, my dear Jamie.'

James pulled a face over her use of his family's nick-name for him, and when Rowan noticed it she almost laughed. She felt oddly lightheaded and the pulse at her temple throbbed so hard it made her feel rather dizzy. But she was not, she vowed, going to be ill now that she had found her grandmother again and had something to celebrate.

'Jamie!' she mocked in a husky whisper, and laughed softly.

James' hand held hers tightly and he looked down at her with the anxiety clearly showing in his eyes. Their bodies were in contact and Rowan was stunningly aware of his nakedness and of the hard strong clasp of his fingers holding her near him.

'I'll give you Jamie!' he murmured harshly close to her ear. 'I'll give you just two minutes to go and get into the bunk your grannie spoke about; just two minutes, mind, and then I'll come and put you into it myself!' He bent his head low, bringing his face close to hers so that his breath warmed her cheek and had a curiously thrilling sensation. 'That's a promise,' he warned.

'But I don't want——'

'Just do as you're told,' James hissed menacingly in her ear. 'I'm going to have a word with Paul, but I'll have my eye on you. And don't think I won't bundle you into yon wee bunk,' he added with an atrociously exaggerated brogue. 'It'd not be the first time I'd——'

'I don't want to know about your sordid exploits!' Rowan interrupted hastily. 'If you think there really is something wrong——'

'There is!'

She accepted his word for it, which might have surprised her in other circumstances, but this was James' world and she had come to trust his judgment in all things pertaining to it. 'I'll tell Grand'mère.' She made that small condition, and he nodded.

'Two minutes,' he warned, and jerked his head in a nod as he turned and moved off into the shadows at the other end of the room to join Paul Ordin.

Seeing him go by and vaguely aware of something going on between her granddaughter and James, Marguerite glanced back over her shoulder, smiling as she got to her feet. 'I need cold water and something to bandage with,' she said, then took note of the shirt Rowan was wearing as if she did so for the first time. 'That shirt is not the most flattering garment for you, my little one,' she told her, then raised a dark brow archly. 'But James is a big man, isn't he?' She did not wait for confirmation but whisked them on to another subject. 'You weren't as lucky as we were finding somewhere to sleep, according to James. It must have been very rough for you, *chérie*.'

'Oh, we managed——' Rowan began, but Réné stepped in quickly with his inevitable complaint.

'It couldn't have been worse,' he told Marguerite. 'We walked and walked and then had to sleep on damp slimy ground and with no proper food. It was sheer purgatory!'

'Oh, René, for heaven's sake stop it!' Rowan heard her own voice as if it was coming from a distance and her head ached more than ever, a sickening curl of nausea rising in her stomach that she hastily sought to subdue while she berated René for his self-pity. 'You're alive, thanks to James, and you've had enough to eat to *keep* you alive, again thanks to James! He brought us here, and you're having your ankle attended to, and again it's thanks to James! Do stop—stop——'

'Rowan!'

She heard James' voice from the other side of the room and saw him start towards her, but she waved her hands to stop him. She wanted to tell him that she was simply tired and needed to rest, but somehow she couldn't move or speak, her legs were far too weak. Her head was burning too and her body felt as if it was on fire, and she was just able to make out softly spoken curses in a familiar voice before she closed her eyes, and the whole thing, sights and sounds, merged into blackness.

CHAPTER SIX

ROWAN tried to focus her wavering gaze on whoever else was in the room, for she felt sure there was someone. Eventually, however, it proved far too much effort, and she could determine very little in the few seconds they re-

mained open. The only impression she gained was of a
small room, dimly shadowed and blessedly cool.   -

Her own body was cooler too, and there was something
wrapped around her in loose folds, clinging and wet and
keeping her arms at her sides. It was in protest at the re-
striction that she jerked her head to one side and made a
barely audible moaning sound. But however faint the
sound she made it brought someone immediately to her
side, and when whoever it was bent over she sensed the
warmth of another body. Then a hand was laid lightly on
her brow, and long gentle fingers smoothed upward, brushing back the dark hair that clung to her forehead.

Again she managed to flutter her eyes open for a second
or two, but the lids felt too heavy and drooped down again
almost at once. Also whoever it was had moved out of her
line of vision to the head of the bed, but an arm slid under-
neath her, lifting her and holding her firm while something, a glass or a cup, was pressed to her lips.

She drank instinctively and gratefully, but the taste
was not what she expected and its strangeness made her
screw up her eyes and purse her mouth in distaste. Shaking
her head from side to side was purely automatic and meant
to avoid the vessel that was once more pressed to her lips.

'Rowan? Drink some more—come on, there's a good
girl.'

It was a man's voice, unidentifiable in her present state
of semi-consciousness, but it was deep and quiet and
definitely authoritative. When she continued to jerk her
head evasively the light hand that had been tucked under
her arm and supporting her was instead curved about her
face and pressed her right cheek to the firm warmth of a
body, while the other pressed the cup against her lips
again, so insistently that they were forced apart and some
of the liquid it held was tipped into her mouth.

'Come on, sweetheart,' the voice coaxed softly. 'Drink

some more of it, don't slip away from me again. Come on now!'

Rowan swallowed some more, simply because she was too listless at the moment to do other than obey, but it tasted no better than the first mouthful had. It was fruity, it was true, but there was some other, as yet unidentifiable, taste that was distinctly unpleasant and which she continued to reject with unreasoning instinct. But the long fingers continued to hold her face firmly and immovably and the only response to her whimper of protest was a momentary light soothing stroke on her cheek.

'I know, I know, it's pretty horrible, isn't it?' The relentless pressure of the cup was in direct contrast to the gentle voice, and it parted her lips again, allowing more of the contents to enter her mouth. 'I hate force-feeding you, my sweet,' the voice went on, 'but we have to get as much of this into you as we can, so it's no good you fighting me.'

Whatever it was that restricted the movement of her arms restricted all her movements, and Rowan simply hadn't the strength to struggle against it. Instead tears of weakness and frustration rolled down her cheeks, and she did not even try to turn away from the next mouthful that passed her lips. When she swallowed it and took another, the voice murmured approvingly and just briefly the encircling arm hugged her.

'*That's* my girl! Come on, sweetheart, another mouthful!'

It was too much effort to even try and talk because her head was spinning and she felt as if she was slowly drifting away from the comforting support of his body. Just briefly something came into her mind, vague and without cause or meaning, and when her lips moved only a whisper of sound emerged. 'Jamie.'

'I'll give you Jamie!' the voice promised, and for a second only she felt the light brush of lips on her brow. 'Open your eyes, my sweet, and swallow some more; come on, Rowan, open your eyes—try hard.'

Rowan tried, she was sure she tried, but she was burning and it was like trying to control the movements of a puppet from a great distance. And before she could achieve it she had slipped once more into oblivion; an oblivion that shut out the despair in James Fraser's voice.

When she next opened her eyes she felt much different. She was much more aware of her surroundings for one thing, although she still felt incredibly weak and the feeling of lassitude alarmed her. For several seconds she lay without moving, looking around the room she was in and quite sure she had never seen it before.

It was small and shadowy and the one window it possessed was merely a square opening without glass, an opening that was made larger by a hole torn in the flimsy fabric of the wall below it. The walls were of wood, and the only item of furniture seemed to be the bunk bed in which she lay, although a packing case stood beside it, just visible from the corner of her eye. There was no sunlight, but a light breeze blew in through the opening; a sultry breeze that was slightly less cool than her own body seemed to be.

It took her several minutes to recall the events that had led to her being there, but one by one the pieces began to fall into place and her brain shed some of its lethargy. She had been reunited with Grand'mère, she remembered, and relived the wonderful moment again in her mind. Then she had indulged in some kind of argument with James, about her being ill or not, something that events had yet again proved him right.

Then, later she thought, someone had forced her to drink something and a quiet, deep gentle voice had murmured softly to her. Whatever it was she had been forced to drink, the taste still lingered and she passed her tongue over dry lips. An attempt to move reminded her of something else too, and she realised that her body was still

swathed in whatever held her arms bound to her sides
and made her virtually helpless.

Just for a second she raised her head and gazed down
at the length of her body. She was wrapped round and
round with what appeared to be miles of grubby white
netting, and it was soaking wet and unpleasantly clammy.
What purpose it served, she could not yet understand, she
knew only that it was horribly uncomfortable and a little
frightening.

'Ah, *chérie*!'

Rowan turned her head when a soft familiar voice penetrated her milling thoughts, and she gazed at her grandmother for a moment with the wide and vaguely blank
eyes of slowly returning consciousness. Marguerite de
Clare's dark eyes shimmered but didn't actually brim tears
and she bent and kissed her, while one hand smoothed
back the hair from her forehead. Emotion gave her normally strong confident voice an unfamiliar huskiness.

'You're feeling better, my darling?' she asked, then
laughed, a light anxious sound, as she answered her own
enquiry. 'But of course you are feeling better; you *look*
better!' Her fingers stroked lightly at Rowan's hair that
clung in damp tendrils to her brow. 'Oh, *ma chérie*, I was
so afraid I would lose you again!'

The stroking movement of her fingers recalled again
that other, half-remembered, moment when other fingers
had moved in that same gentle caressing motion over her
forehead. 'Who——' She passed the tip of her tongue
over her lips and tried again. 'Who was here before?'

'Before?' Marguerite smiled down at her, reaching with
one hand for something that stood on the packing case beside the bed. 'You have to drink lots of this, *petite*, it is
to help you get better. It tastes awful, but it's necessary
for you to drink litres and litres of it, my child.'

The sight of the handleless cup in her hand again
jogged Rowan's memory and a small frown drew her brows

together. 'He—he made me drink it,' she insisted, and clung for a moment to the very hazy recollection of a supporting arm and a broad comforting chest; a deep voice that murmured endearments to encourage her, and the light touch of lips on her brow.

She had no need to ask who it was who had visited her and held her tightly while he forced her to drink some revolting brew that she could still taste even though the incident itself was only a hazy recollection. Marguerite did not question her meaning, but slipped an arm beneath her, raising her a little, but with much less ease than her earlier caller had done.

'I owe James so very much,' Marguerite said, holding the cup for her to drink from. 'I wouldn't have known what on earth to do for you if he hadn't been here, and heaven knows what would have happened. He knew what to do—and not only that, he's so efficient at adapting to his environment. He made use of what little we had available and even concocted this awful brew for you. You must drink it, Rowan, because it's essential for your recovery.'

Rowan was thirsty and longed for something to drink, but in view of what her grandmother had said and taking her own vague recollection into account, she eyed the cup that Marguerite offered without enthusiasm. The liquid it contained was orange in colour and looked refreshing enough, but still she swallowed the first mouthful cautiously.

'The fruit disguises it a little,' Marguerite suggested, much as she had once stated the redeeming features of foods she had disliked as a child. 'I know it can't be nice at all, *chérie*, but there's nothing else we can give you that serves the same purpose. You lost so much fluid through sweating as you did in that wretched jungle.'

Rowan pulled a face. She had no doubt that if she was being given the dreadful stuff it was essential to her recovery, but she was thirsty and the unmistakable tang of salt repelled her. She turned her head from the proferred cup and pulled a face, hating the weakness that again brought her to the brink of tears. 'Grand'mère, I'm parched and you want me to drink salt water!'

'You must, child.' Marguerite sat on the edge of the bed and put the cup to her lips coaxingly. 'James says it's essential for you to have it.'

Rowan's lip trembled and with a sigh of resignation her grandmother laid her gently back and stood looking down at her. Marguerite de Clare was so seldom at a loss, but she had never been so much out of her element before and she had a great deal to cope with. Self-reproach made Rowan want to reach up and take her hand, but that too was denied her and she shook her head helplessly.

'I'm sorry, Grand'mère,' she whispered.

'Is everything O.K., Maggie?'

A well remembered voice broke into the uneasy silence and Rowan's heart gave a distinct jolt, then began to thud hard, and there was a curious tightening sensation in her stomach as she looked past her grandmother at the tall figure that stood in the doorway.

'Is she conscious again?' James enquired, and came across the tiny room soft-footed as a cat, to stand towering over her.

In the brief time she had Rowan noticed that he was wearing his shirt again, his broad shoulders and chest filling it much more completely than her own slender shape had done. There was anxiety in the ice-blue eyes that looked down at her for a moment, then they warmed with a smile that was echoed by a glimpse of strong teeth, and Rowan accepted gratefully the satisfactory glow of familiarity it gave her.

'So you're back with us again!' he said.

Rowan lowered her eyes until the fringe of her lashes fanned like dark crescents on her cheeks. Bound as she was in yards of netting she was weak and unnervingly vulnerable, and she wished James need not have seen her like that, although heaven knew why it mattered. He looked enormous in the small room and yet there was something so reassuring about his looming over her as he did that she felt suddenly much less tearful and unhappy.

'I don't want to drink salt water,' she whispered in a small, plaintive voice, and James' sudden short bark of laughter was so unexpected that she flicked her eyes open wide and stared up at him.

'Oh yes, you're getting back to normal, thank God!' His rolling r's sent little thrills of sensation right down her spine, and Rowan noticed how her grandmother was smiling at him. 'Well, whatever you want or don't want, my girl, you're going to drink this stuff. If you're very good I'll bring you some plain orange juice for a treat, but it's absolutely imperative that you put back all the salt and fluid you've lost the past couple of days.'

'I know, James, but if I could——'

'No buts,' James interrupted firmly. 'Your grannie and I have worked like slaves preparing this concoction for you and I'll not have you turning up your pretty nose at it simply because it doesn't taste like champagne!' He leaned over her and Rowan noticed how her grandmother moved back to allow him to get closer. 'Nor am I going to stand by and see you waste away after all the trouble it's been getting you this far. So—just you make up your mind to it, girl! You're going to get through gallons and gallons of that devil's brew or I'll know the reason why.'

'You're *still* a bully!'

Her defiance was barely more than a whisper and only half-hearted at that. She glanced at her grandmother, but for once Marguerite was apparently content to yield her authority to a stronger personality and all she did was smile and nod encouragingly.

'Now,' said James, 'are you going to take it from Maggie or from me?'

The decision was made for her when Marguerite silently handed him the cup, and Rowan's heart gave a great lurch in her breast when she saw the way he smiled. She struggled for a moment, trying to free her hands, but as she fought against the binding folds of net, she realised something. She had obviously been stripped before being wrapped in it, and it was a gauzy glimpse of her own nakedness that made her stop.

Instead she let herself go limp when James thrust an arm under her and raised her from the bed. It was so easy and so instinctive to lean against him, snugly tucked between his encircling arm and the warmth of his body in the towelling shirt they seemed to take turns in wearing. 'You took it back,' she murmured when she noticed, and the throbbing vibration of his laughter rippled through her.

'You can have it back again when you're up and about,' he promised. 'For now you don't need anything more than your bridal gown!'

'It's the mosquito netting that was left behind,' Marguerite told her. 'We hadn't a sheet, so we soaked the net in the stream outside and wrapped you in that. It's the accepted way to bring down a temperature in cases like yours, so James tells me, and it certainly seems to have worked for you, *chérie*, eh?'

All the time James was tipping the orange and salt water into her mouth, Rowan mulled over the latest information, and there were things about the situation that she found hard to accept calmly. Her grandmother was a well built woman, and quite capable, but it would be no easy task to wrap a completely inert body in all those folds of netting, as neatly and efficiently as Rowan was wrapped.

She looked at Marguerite with slightly evasive eyes as she paused for breath, and wondered if the suddenly more rapid beat of her heart would be detected by the fingers that rested just under her breast. She dared not look up into the face that hovered over her, waiting to pour more of the foul-tasting drink into her, but she looked down at the folds of mosquito net and at the hint of her own pale flesh beneath it.

It was uncanny the way James could sometimes come in on her thoughts and Rowan found it appallingly discomfiting that he did so now. His voice was quiet and matter-of-fact, gently understanding in contrast to the brusque words he used. 'In a case of emergency it was no time to worry about your girlish modesty, my sweet; Maggie couldn't manage it alone.'

Her heart responded with such violence that there was no doubt he noticed it this time and the long hard fingers curved more tightly for a moment, squeezing her to him in a kind of forceful caress that was alarmingly disturbing. Rowan turned her head from the pressure of the cup on her lips only a moment afterwards, obeying instinct rather than consciously defiant, but James followed her move, firm and insistent.

'Take some more, Rowan, you haven't had nearly enough yet.'

'It's foul!' She made the protest breathlessly after swallowing a mouthful, and struggled against the supporting arm. 'Give me time to get my breath, James! I—I can't keep drinking without pause—without taking a breath sometimes.'

She hated feeling weak and helpless and especially while James held her as he did. The sight of her own barely concealed nakedness was a reminder of just how vulnerable she was, and when she turned her face into the curve of his shoulder it was partly in frustration and partly some emotion she was at a complete loss to understand. But there was something so reassuringly familiar about being there that she went on hiding her face and did not even consider what her grandmother might be thinking, while James stroked a hand over her hair and rested his chin lightly on the top of her head.

'Come on, girl, try some more now.' His voice was quiet and soothing, but it was relentless too in its intent, and Rowan thought rather wildly that he would probably be just as firm and unyielding even with a woman he loved. 'Just another wee sip,' he coaxed, 'and then I'll let you rest for a while. After that, if your temperature stays down and you go on as you are, we'll wrap you in something dry and more comfortable.'

Rowan gulped down more of the hateful stuff, then glanced up at his face, meeting the light eyes head on and finding them more disturbing than she would have believed possible. The creases at their corners were much easier to see at close quarters, fanning out like a fine web in the darkly tanned skin, and there was a glimpse of something in their depths that stirred her emotions alarmingly.

She hadn't noticed her grandmother going, and only vaguely registered the fact that she was no longer with them when she skimmed her gaze over the dark, familiar face above her and was aware of the close, intimate silence in the room. Whether or not Marguerite's presence would have made any difference was debatable, and when James brought his face down to hers, she lifted her mouth eagerly.

But his kiss was gentle and not a bit like the last time he had kissed her. There was nothing of passion or impulse in this instance, only a light tender caress that teased her senses without satisfying them. Even so it set her heart hammering so hard that she felt as if it would stop or burst from her body, and she closed her eyes as she leaned against him, bound with the strong curve of his arm.

'You're in no state to be kissed,' James murmured against her ear, and his lips brushed her forehead lightly. 'I'll leave you to rest for a while and then Maggie can take off this clammy outfit and put you into something more comfortable.'

'I can dress?' Her head was swimming and she didn't

know whether to blame James' kiss or her own weakness for it.

'You can swap a wet wrapping for a dry one,' James promised. 'But you still have to keep swigging this jungle juice for quite a while yet, and keep still and cool. I'll keep a close watch on your temperature and if it starts rising again we'll have to go back to the cold wet treatment again.'

'James——'

'Sssh!' He pressed his lips to her forehead, then laid her back on the bed again, the touch of his big hands incredibly gentle. 'You keep quiet and rest. Ah-ah!' He silenced another attempt to speak and Rowan looked up at him reproachfully from her prone position.

Watching him cross the tiny room she felt a curious mingling of emotions that was utterly confusing, and once more that strange curling sensation fluttered in her stomach. She could just manage to move her hands under the folds of mosquito netting, and she slid them as far as she could down the smooth curve of her thighs. Just thinking about how she came to be wound so neatly in the cooling sheet brought a leaping urgency to her pulse and added fire to the heat of her body, but there was a faint smile on her mouth as she closed her eyes and let herself relax.

When Rowan woke next it was with the certainty that she was feeling very much better, and she turned her head with animated interest when she caught sight of a movement from the corner of her eye. Her heart was already beating faster and there was a smile on her face as she anticipated James' return to check on her progress.

But instead it was René's head that poked through the doorless aperture, his round eyes darting a hasty glance backwards before he ventured into the room. He looked paler than she remembered and, inevitably she supposed, slightly sulky, so that his appearance did less to cheer her than James' would have done. Nevertheless she smiled at him in a way that encouraged him to come right into the room, noting how awkwardly he hobbled on his one good foot.

'Rowan! My darling!' He spoke low and half under his breath, and made it obvious that he did not want to be overheard, making Rowan wonder how many times since she became ill he had been denied access to her on James' instructions. He dropped on to the edge of her bed, and eyes surveyed her anxiously. 'Oh, my sweet darling, how are you?'

'Much better, René, thank you.'

She wished he need not look quite so harassed and anxious, but she had soon realised that René found it impossible to be himself in this strange and rather savage environment. 'If only I'd known how ill you were!' He did not hesitate to take advantage of her prone position and the fact that she couldn't do a thing to prevent him even had she wanted to, and he kissed her full on her mouth, a long lingering kiss that left her alarmingly short of breath. 'Oh, my darling, they wouldn't let me come near you and I've been worried sick!'

'I'm sorry.' It amazed her to realise that she didn't know quite what to say to him, and although she was feeling very much better, she was still astonishingly weak and languorous. 'How's your ankle?' she asked, and René shook his head. Very obviously his capacity for self-pity was undiminished, however concerned he was for her.

'It hurts like hell,' he stated unhesitatingly. 'But there hasn't been much time to spare for a sprained ankle with you so ill, my love.'

'Oh, poor René!'

'Oh, it didn't matter, of course,' he assured her hastily, and looked vaguely uneasy for a second or two before he went on. 'It wasn't that so much that I minded, it was being

—left out. I don't know that I could have done anything
towards healing you, but I could have sat with you and
held your hand; and I'd have been much happier if
Madame hadn't laid such great store by James' ability as
a doctor. He simply took over.'

It was incredible, Rowan thought, how he could so
determinedly find cause to blame James for just about
everything unpleasant that happened to them. 'It was the
sensible thing to do,' Rowan pointed out. 'James is the only
one with any experience of this kind of thing, and Grand'-
mère needed his help.'

'Very convenient!' René jeered, and perhaps for the
first time Rowan took a real good look at him as he really
was.

Undoubtedly he was good-looking and while they were
aboard the yacht he had been charming enough to sweep
any girl off her feet. She had found him attractive, and
to some extent she still did, but there was so much more
she noticed about him now—for one thing, the fact that
the good-looking features had a certain weakness, and that
his full mouth had an almost permanently petulant pout.
René was rich and handsome and spoiled and not in the
habit of making the best of any situation that did not
exactly fit his requirements.

Just the same Rowan felt sorry for him rather than
blamed him, and it was discomfiting to realise she had
something to do with his unhappiness too. For weeks,
while they were aboard the *Belle o' Dunoon*, she had
listened to him extol the virtues of his good friend James
Fraser, and remained unconverted. Yet in only a few days
their respective opinions had been completely reversed,
and René must find it as difficult to understand as she did
herself.

Sitting on the bed, René took note of her slender shape
encased in a cocoon of mosquito net, and she saw his frown
when he noticed the unmistakable shimmer of pale flesh

through its texture. Even so he did not shift his gaze from the sight that his expression suggested he disapproved of, and she waited for his comment.

'What's the idea of the winding sheet?'

'To bring my temperature down.' Rowan knew only as much as Marguerite had told her, but she passed on the information for what it was worth, though it did nothing to pacify him, judging by his expression. 'It's the accepted treatment, apparently.'

'So James says!' René swore suddenly and thumped a hand on the packing case so forcefully that it threatened to collapse. 'Damn it, I saw him bring that damned stuff in here, wringing wet, but I'd no idea—*He* put it round you, didn't he?'

'He helped Grand'mère—she couldn't manage alone, I was completely dead weight.' René swore again and his voice grated on Rowan's nerves, making her head throb warningly so that she closed her eyes briefly. 'Don't, René, please,' she begged. 'My head still aches and——'

'He had no *right*!' René insisted, ignoring her plea, and Rowan's voice rose too, in protest.

'Would you rather he'd let me die?' she demanded, then swallowed hard when she realised just how weak she was still. 'Please—don't be silly, René. James only did what had to be done, and I'm sure he had far too much on his mind to think about—what you have in mind.'

'I don't believe it! And anyway I don't see——'

'I don't see why you didn't leave Rowan to rest as she's supposed to do,' said James from the doorway, and he came across with that long and deceptively lazy stride, bringing up at the bedside as René got up.

There was a wary, mistrustful look in his blue eyes and Rowan felt the tension between the two of them as she lay there helpless and suddenly fearful for no good reason she could think of. 'James——' she ventured.

'Temperature check,' he told her in a firmly practical

voice, and she noticed then that he had a clinical thermometer in one hand.

She automatically opened her mouth and allowed him to pop it under her tongue, then studied him from the concealment of her lashes, while René stood by, awkward on his injured ankle but apparently prepared to defy any suggestion that he should leave.

'Every mod con!' he jeered, referring to the thermometer, and James cocked a light brow at him.

'Unfortunately not,' he denied with studied coolness. 'It would have been much less touch and go if we *had* had every modern convenience.' René made no response, and after a time James retrieved the thermometer and frowned over its reading before shaking it back to normal. 'Still falling,' he remarked, and gave Rowan an encouraging smile. 'I'll tell Maggie she can wrap you in a dry sheet.' His hand rested lightly on the curve of her hip for a moment, and the warmth of his palm through the texture of the netting jolted her senses alarmingly. 'It'll be a bit more comfortable than this stuff,' he suggested.

Rowan kept the thickness of her lashes between her own evasive eyes and the steady, almost challenging, look in James'. 'What are you going to use this time?' she asked, and missed the hint of smile that touched a corner of his mouth for a moment.

'*I'm* not going to use anything, girl,' he told her. 'Maggie can manage in this instance, I think.' It was automatic to glance up when he reached out a hand and placed it very lightly on her forehead, and she noticed he was nodding his head. 'You're not on fire any more,' he said, 'but I'm going to have to tip some more of this jungle juice into you; we can't afford to have you dry out again or we'll be back to square one.'

'Oh, James, must you?'

Her voice was plaintive, but Rowan did not expect him to be influenced by it in the least, and she noticed the way he smiled. 'Yes, I must, Rowan. You're a long way from being fully recovered yet, and I'm not taking any chances on you having a relapse.' He edged his way between René and the bed and reached for the cup of orange. 'Come on now, sweetheart, don't go temperamental on me.'

'*Damn* you!'

René's indignant curse seemed to startle him, for he half-turned and looked at him with raised brows, the cup still in his hand. '*Now* what?' he enquired mildly.

'You know damned well!' René told him.

His face was flushed and there was a glint in his eyes that implied he found it hard to believe he had heard aright. It wasn't easy to affect a dignified stance when he had to balance on one foot, but he achieved it quite well by using the support of the wall behind him. He was shaking with anger and his hands were clenched into tight fists that he pressed hard against the supporting wall.

'For one thing I object to you calling Rowan sweetheart, and for another, I'm perfectly capable of giving her whatever concoction you've been pouring into her! You've done your expert act with the thermometer, now get out and let me take care of Rowan, the way it should be!'

The atmosphere was tense, taut as a bow-string, and Rowan felt helpless to take any part in the exchange. Flat on her back and bound hand and foot as she was, there was little she could do, but she held her breath waiting for James to react, her heart thudding hard when he turned very slowly and placed the full cup back on the packing case. There was a lazy, almost sensual slowness in his movements that suggested a temper held firmly in check.

'By all means!' The same dangerous calm was in his voice too, but perhaps only Rowan recognised it, for René was hot with his own anger and wary of any and every move he made, a man who sensed a too easy victory and mistrusted it. 'You look after her, René!'

'You think I'm not capable?' René demanded, but somehow did not quite meet the light, steady gaze that was fixed on him.

'That remains to be seen,' James told him. 'But be quite sure you *do* look after her, because if she has a relapse or anything goes wrong, I'm going to take you apart piece by piece, my friend, and feed you to the sharks. O.K.?' He asked it so softly that Rowan shivered.

René looked as if he did not quite believe it. He looked stunned by both the quiet menace of the threat and by the change in the man he had thought he knew so well. He seemed to recover himself quite quickly, however, and a brief nod accepted responsibility as he turned and picked up the cup. 'I'll cope,' he said, and turned his back.

But although René might have been satisfied with the arrangement, Rowan was in two minds about her own feelings, and she followed James' tall figure as far as the door, with anxious eyes. 'James!'

She wasn't even sure what had made her call out to him, but he turned at once and the look in his eyes brought a swift urgency to her heartbeat. It was a bright, expectant look that she did not understand until it was too late. He gave her a second or two to follow through, then smiled faintly and waved a hand in careless salute.

'See you later, girl,' he told her. 'You'll be fine if you just keep swigging that jungle cocktail.'

He was already gone before Rowan realised the meaning of that look. He had expected her to call him back, to insist that he carried on treating her, and Rowan did not altogether understand her own bitter frustration because she had failed to realise it.

The information that Paul Ordin had high hopes of being able to repair the radio before very long had been a definite morale booster, and Rowan was anxious to prove herself fit again. Also she was tired of being in bed and being inactive. It wasn't as if she was at home and could indulge herself in luxuries.

There was little comfort in the tiny bunk bed, and she knew that her grandmother had occupied it the night before their arrival. It seemed wrong somehow for her to have the only bed while Marguerite had to make do with one of the chairs, and it added to her unrest.

'Surely I've been here long enough?' She tried not to sound complaining, but didn't quite succeed. 'I'm better now, James, and I can't see any reason for you keeping me here.'

'By brute force?' he suggested, and his eyes mocked her from the far end of the bed. 'I suppose you're bored stiff?'

'I feel lazy,' Rowan told him. 'It can't be easy finding food for us all and preparing it, and I've done nothing but lie here.'

Seemingly lazy blue eyes watched her steadily with a gleaming warmth in their depths that she always found so disturbing. 'You're very good at doing nothing and looking decorative,' he informed her. 'And when you do get up you're not going to start dashing around and bringing on a relapse; but if you're getting restless maybe you could get up and move around a little bit. I'll take your temperature and see if you're still normal.'

'I am!'

He noticed the confidence with which she expressed herself and eyed her for a minute in silence. She was covered by a curtain that had once draped the open doorway of the bedroom, wrapped around her and tucked in, her shoulders bare and resting against the wall behind the bed. Hands clasped together in front of her, she met his eyes uneasily, on the defensive before she knew for certain whether she had reason to be.

'René got me the thermometer and I took my own temperature,' she told him. 'It didn't matter, my borrowing it, did it, James?'

'Not in the least.' It was the voice she had learned not to take at face value, and she stirred restlessly. 'But you won't mind if I check for myself, will you?'

He was gone only a few seconds and when he returned she went through the now automatic routine, holding the thermometer in her mouth while he stood with a hand on her forehead, much too close for her comfort and making her pulse hammer feverishly. There was a vigorous maleness about James that she had never discovered in any other man, and it was infinitely disturbing in the circumstances.

Glancing up at him was compulsive and she found his eyes on her, steady and alarmingly expressive so that her pulse became even more agitated. The long fingers resting on her brow smoothed back her hair then moved along her hairline with a touch like a caress, continuing down her cheek and to her neck, her eyes held the whole time by that unwavering blue gaze.

He seemed to recover himself suddenly, and retrieved the thermometer from her lips with some semblance of his more practical normality, and examined it. 'You'll do,' he announced, and Rowan blinked at him for a moment uncertainly.

'Do you mean I'm all right?' Relief and pleasure dawned slowly, bringing to her grey eyes a warmer, deeper glow. 'That I can shed this blasted curtain and put my clothes on?'

'You can shed that blasted curtain and put *my* clothes on,' James corrected her with a faint smile. 'Or my shirt anyway, though you'd better not do either until I'm gone or René'll be throwing a jealous tantrum, and I don't think I could face that at the moment.'

It often surprised her how well she could read him, and she sensed something amiss now, eyeing him curiously as she sat curled up on the bed. 'What's gone wrong, James?' she asked, and he arched a swift brow at her.

'How do you know——'

'I can tell,' Rowan interrupted quickly. 'What is it, James?'

He sat himself on the foot of the bed, running both hands through the thick tawny mane of his hair before he answered her. 'Nothing much, I suppose,' he said. 'Paul thought he had the radio problem licked and now he hasn't, that's all.' It didn't sound much said like that, but it could mean the difference between life and eventual slow death if they weren't found quite soon. Rowan recognised it and James saw the realisation in her eyes. Reaching out, he stroked a hand down her cheek and it was quite instinctive when she leaned her face into the warm curve of his palm. 'He'll come up with the solution, sweetheart, don't worry,' he murmured. 'It won't last forever.'

'I know.'

She felt she could quite happily have stayed like that, with her cheek resting in James' hand, for he had the gift of being able to shut out the unpleasant possibilities and inspire her flagging spirits with optimism. But such unproductive pleasantries weren't encouraged for very long, and he got to his feet again, looking down at her curled up against the wall.

'I wish there was something else I could wear instead of your shirt,' Rowan said, and he regarded her curiously.

'Have you got something against wearing my shirt all of a sudden?'

Already she could imagine the warmth of his body touching her own skin and a curious fluttering in her stomach deepened her rate of breathing as she shook her head. 'No, of course I haven't, but I don't like leaving you shirtless with all those mosquitoes about.'

'Och away!' James told her with an exaggeration of his brogue he sometimes affected. 'Maggie likes to admire my manly torso, she'll be thankful I've parted with it again.'

It was so very likely to be true that Rowan laughed, and was still laughing when René appeared. He took in the fact of their laughing and of their being together with the inevitable glowering look of dislike, and he moved across the room towards them, hobbling painfully. 'Isn't it wonderful,' Rowan called out the moment she saw him, 'James says I'm fit to get up and get dressed?'

'Wearing his shirt again, I suppose?' René guessed, and Rowan felt a flick of impatience as she kept a firm hold on her temper.

'I haven't much option,' she told him, 'unless I wear this curtain like a sarong. Is that what you'd rather I did?'

René simply looked sulky, but just for a moment Rowan caught James' eye, and she could not imagine what made him look so devilish suddenly. His light blue eyes gleamed wickedly and his teeth were bared in a smile that sent shivers through her. 'It's a very interesting idea,' he said in those quietly rolling tones that could have such an effect. 'But regardless of what Hollywood does, girl, the correct way to wear a sarong is from the waist down, leaving the breasts naked.' He gave René a brief and slightly malicious glance, noting his stunned expression, then shook his head as he turned away. 'I don't think that would go down very well in the present situation, do you?'

René was glaring at him, and, suspecting he was gathering his objections for an argument Rowan stepped in quickly, calling after James as he made for the door, 'Aren't you going to leave me your shirt, James?'

Without a word he stripped it off and flung it across to her, and just briefly as she held the warmth of his body in her arms, he caught her eye again. 'Sorry it hasn't been washed first,' he said quietly, and watched for a moment the colour that flooded into her face.

She murmured her thanks, then turned to René, sulky and stubborn and looking as if he meant to stay. 'If you'll just give me a minute, René, I'll get dressed.'

His dark, morose eyes scanned her face for a moment and settled on her bare shoulders before sweeping down to where the makeshift sarong was tucked in over her left breast. 'You didn't mind him seeing you——' he began, but Rowan cut him short.

'Of course I minded!' She was more sensitive about James' part in helping to wrap her in the necessary cold sheet needed for treating her initially than she cared to admit, and she hated René for reminding her of it. 'That was unavoidable, but I don't propose putting on a peepshow for you or anyone else, René. You can either leave or I'll stay as I am!'

He resented it, that was clear, but obviously he saw himself with little option, and he thrust out his lip in dislike. 'I'll wait outside,' he said, and gave her a sharp and narrow-eyed look before he hobbled over to the door. 'Just in case anyone comes snooping around while you're dressing.'

When he had left her, Rowan looked across at the gaping hole under the window and the window with no glass, and shrugged resignedly. The room had no door and there was no guarantee that she wouldn't be overlooked by someone, but privacy was a commodity that was in short supply in the present situation. Sooner or later she had the feeling that the lack of it was going to cause more dissension, and she could only hope that Paul Ordin's skill with the radio would enable them to get away before it happened. It was all any of them could hope for.

CHAPTER SEVEN

It was with James' warning in mind that Rowan took things easily for the next few days. They were all becoming listless and too easily tired, and their diet of fruit was only occasionally varied with fish that either James or Paul managed to catch. So far no one's morale had broken down, but the endless frustration of their own helplessness was beginning to tell, and René particularly was increasingly morose and uncommunicative.

Rowan would like to have gone with James when he went foraging for their food, but he refused to take her and forbade Paul to. Fetching water from the stream, however, was a different matter and he took her along with him, letting her carry the battered zinc pail that was all they had for fetching and storing their water.

The stream ran only about a hundred metres from the hut and at the very edge of the clearing, and James' suggestion that it was an offshoot of the spring that had provided their first day bath seemed a logical one. It was cool and clean and provided all the fresh water they needed, and although it was much closer to the sea than the other had been, it too was untainted by salt.

At this end of the island too, the sea was much closer and more accessible, for only a narrow band of vegetation cut them off from a sandy bay very similar to the one they had fetched up on originally, and was hemmed in by the same density of undergrowth. Clearly it would have been the means of access for the original occupant of the hut, and Rowan sometimes pondered on what had become of him. It was his possible fate that gave her occasional shivers of uneasiness when the shifting silence of the jungle crept in with the darkness each night.

Activity of any kind, even being allowed to carry the water pail to the stream, was welcome, but having done that Rowan discovered she was to be delegated to the role of onlooker. 'Why can't I do that?' she asked, when James took the pail from her, and he shook his head.

'Because standing in the sun, bent double, isn't the best thing for someone still recovering from heat-stroke,' he told her. 'You just sit and look decorative and talk to me while I do the work.'

While not at all averse to being cosseted, Rowan felt obliged to make some kind of response, if only on principle. 'I'm not really fragile, you know,' she said, sitting herself down on the bank of the stream. 'You don't have to treat me as if you think I'll melt away just doing a simple job like filling a bucket with water.'

James' ice-blue eyes looked at her steadily for a moment, and there was that look in them that always made her senses react in the most alarming way. 'Och, you love being coddled and cared for,' he insisted, his r's rolling softly. 'You know you do, Rowan. Be honest, eh?'

Smiling was irresistible, just as tilting up her chin was, and she shook her hair forward by bending her head. It helped hide her face as she clasped her hands around her knees and hugged them to her. 'All right,' she admitted, 'I *do*! So I'll just sit here and let you do all the work.'

'That's my girl!'

Rowan chose to ignore the faintly paternalistic approval, and contented herself with watching him as he dispensed with his sandals and stepped ankle-deep into the water. The stream was too shallow to allow the bucket itself to be filled by simply immersing it, so it was necessary to use a small tin basin and do it by degrees. It was a process that called for a great deal of patience, but patience was something that James had in abundance, he had proved that often enough.

It still intrigued Rowan that he seemed to conform so well to his surroundings, and yet had been equally at home amid the luxury on board the yacht. More often than she cared to remember, she had made allowances for René because he came from a background of wealth and comfort, but it seldom occurred to her that the same yardstick could be used in James' case.

Musing secretly to herself, Rowan rested her chin on her arms and regarded him through her lashes while he repeatedly dipped the tin basin into the stream and emptied it into the pail. He came from a background at least as affluent as René's, and could enjoy the same comforts, but it had taken an enforced exile on a deserted island to stress the yawning chasm of difference between them, where once they had seemed so similar.

René, in his own environment, was smooth and confidently charming, as James was, but James it seemed could flourish equally well in this much less civilised world too. Of course it had to do with temperament, but she wondered if perhaps René did not apply himself so diligently to the task of adapting. Whichever it was, Rowan was convinced she would not have survived if her safety had depended upon René alone.

'How long have you known René, James?'

She asked the question out of the blue and inevitably James was curious, looking up for a moment with his eyes narrowed against the sun. 'I met him about six, seven years ago when we moved into the French market; our fathers had dealings and we just took it from there.' He glanced up again and his eyes quizzed her. 'Are you checking on his background? I can assure you his pedigree's impeccable!'

'Don't be nasty, James!'

He was again concentrating on what he was doing, or so it appeared, but he didn't let the matter drop as Rowan rather hoped he would. Her initial enquiry had been more concerned with how he and René came to be friends than with her own relationship with René, and she had found that brief quizzical look very disconcerting because of the things it suggested.

'Sorry,' he said. 'I didn't know I was. Why the curiosity?'

'I just—wondered, that's all. You seem such different characters to have become friends.'

He seemed to muse on that for several seconds, then he glanced up and half-smiled, making it difficult to guess what his feelings were. 'Don't judge by present standards, Rowan,' he told her eventually. 'We've been good friends, but it's the kind of friendship that's never had to stand against exactly these kind of conditions before.'

Rowan could find no answer to that because she remembered how René had complained so self-pityingly about James never having cheated him with a woman before. It became an embarrassingly personal matter the way James took it, and she was suddenly anxious to drop it, changing the subject with somewhat breathless haste.

'How do you know this *is* an island, James? Have you been here before?'

He looked up, for longer this time, and his eyes searched her flushed face for a second or two before he answered her. 'I've sailed in this part of the world before,' he told her, 'although I have to admit that right at this moment I couldn't place our situation to a mile or two. I have only our last reading to go by, and we weren't near anything but a few islands, mostly uninhabited. Don't worry, girl,' he added in that stunningly affecting voice, 'we're not so far off the shipping lanes that our call won't be picked up.'

'Oh, I'm not worried.'

'Good!'

Rowan wondered if he actually believed her, or if his seeming offhandedness was meant to encourage her. While she was still pondering on it, he straightened up, standing with his bare feet planted firmly on the bed of the stream. Wearing only a pair of thin cotton slacks that constant immersion had shrunk until they fitted like a second skin, he was an alarmingly disturbing figure, and again Rowan felt that curious sensation in her stomach.

'Don't sit out there in the full sun,' he told her, apparently unaware of the effect he was having, 'you'll be passing out on me again, and I couldn't go through all that again!'

'I'm all right,' Rowan insisted, but then placed a hand on the top of her head automatically and found it far hotter than she expected.

'It's hot already, isn't it?' James said, and obviously had no doubt at all.

'A bit, that's all.'

She admitted it only reluctantly, but James was shaking his head at her. 'Get back to the shack,' he told her, 'or else move back into the shade. Use your sense, you daft wee creature, instead of risking heat-stroke again. Go on, move back into the shade!'

Showing an astonishing readiness to comply, Rowan uncurled herself, but moved back only far enough to be out of the direct sun, then once more settled down to watch him take up his leisurely task of scooping up water to fill the pail. Hugging her knees tightly, she looked across at him with a curious sense of excitement stirring in her that was quite inexplicable at the moment.

'Were you always so bossy?' she asked, uncaring about how provocatively she worded it, and when James looked up again one fair brow was cocked at her in a way that suggested a warning. 'Grand'mère says you're a Leo man,' she went on heedlessly, 'and they're naturally bossy; it's one of their traits.'

'If I remember rightly,' James corrected her with deceptive quietness, 'Maggie's version was somewhat different. She says that Leo men have the quality of leadership.' He looked at her with a suddenly challenging gleam in his eyes. 'That's not quite the same thing, is it?'

It rather surprised Rowan that she accepted the rebuke without comment, but nothing about her present mood was easily explainable at the moment. Sitting with her hands clasped around her legs, she gazed at the sun sparkling and dancing on the surface of the water and felt a desire to wallow in its silky soft coolness. It was a curiously sensual desire that was not entirely unconnected with the tall, virile figure that stood so patiently collecting water, and she did little to subdue it.

'The water looks very inviting,' she ventured, and James looked at her curiously for a moment.

'It's hardly deep enough to bathe in, and I'd have thought you'd had enough of being wet.'

'Oh, I've had enough of being half-drowned, and of being wound up like a mummy in mosquito netting,' she allowed, and caught his eye. 'But as you said, it isn't quite the same thing, is it?'

James smiled lazily and tipped water into the almost full bucket. 'Mebbe not,' he allowed, 'but I'd as soon you didn't dunk yourself in the drinking water right at this moment.'

Wrinkling her nose at him by way of reproach was the only response she made, but she continued to watch him. There was something so ruggedly earthy about James that could sometimes even make her forget that they were stranded miles from anywhere, and in a potentially dangerous situation. He was not only adaptable himself, but he had the ability to bring something of the same quality to her as well, and she sometimes felt she must pull herself up sharply when she fell to studying him as she was now. Which was why she sought a distraction.

'Is it possible that something from the *Belle* might eventually get washed ashore?' she asked, and he raised his head briefly, as if her motive interested him more than the question itself.

'I've thought about that,' he confessed. 'Now that you're up and about again I might scout around further along the coast, among the trees. Not that I've any intention of taking you with me,' he added quickly when he correctly interpreted a half-formed question, 'but it's possible there might be something to be salvaged that we can't see from the bay.'

'Something that might help Paul mend the radio?'

James shrugged. 'Maybe.'

'He—he's not getting on very well with it, is he?'

The slight tremor in her voice was barely detectable, but James noticed it and glanced up again. 'I've complete trust in Paul,' he told her. 'If it can be done, then Paul's the man to do it.'

The question hovered on her lips for several seconds before she found the courage to ask it. 'And if he can't?'

Once more he heaved his broad shoulders resignedly. 'I don't know, girl.'

'But you *must* know!' Rowan protested. Never before had she heard him sound even vaguely unsure of anything, and hearing it now, panic surged upward and soured her mouth. Her heart thudded urgently and there was a wide, blank look in her eyes as she stared at his bent head. 'It's not like you to admit you don't know the answer to anything,' she told him, half accusing and not for a moment realising how unreasonable she was being. 'You've known all along what to do and how to cope with everything; I've got to rely on you, James, and I—I don't think I can accept that you're fallible!'

James straightened up, and just for a moment he stood looking across at her with such a curiously intent gaze that it sent shivers along her spine. Then he stepped out of the water and bent to pull on his sandals, struggling against the drag of wet feet on leather soles, before rubbing his hands slowly up and down the legs of his slacks to dry them, as if he did it automatically.

When he looked at her again, his eyes were darkly shadowed by their heavy lashes. 'You have to allow me fallibility, Rowan,' he said, and the very softness of his voice was an appeal. 'I'm a man, not a computer, and I make mistakes; there are things I can't answer truthfully without giving away the fact that I'm human.'

'James——?'

'I've every reason to believe Paul can get that radio going and that we'll eventually get off this blasted swamp, but please, in God's name, don't take my word as gospel —make allowances for me, as you do for René.'

'James, I'm sorry!'

Her voice was small and a sheen of tears showed in the misty greyness of her eyes as she looked up at him. Then he reached out a hand to her, the long brown fingers half flexed and proving an irresistible lure. Rowan moved across and placed her own hand into it, making no demur when he squeezed it so tightly that her fingers were crushed. She could feel the hard, throbbing beat of her own pulse when by some slight movement she brought brief contact between their two bodies, and her lips parted with the faint breath of sound she made in the moment she glanced up at him.

His eyes had the bright, searing heat of diamonds, light and gleaming between their heavy lashes, and his free hand reached out and slipped beneath her left arm, the broad palm pressing warmly to the curve of her breast. Rowan moved towards him as if by some irresistible force, and the quivering tenseness of her body seemed to curve towards him as if of its own volition.

His face, rugged and dark below his mane of tawny hair, loomed above her and she half-closed her eyes, acting on some instinct she had no control over. Then her mouth, soft and moist-lipped, turned up to the promise of passion that gave a firm, almost cruel look to his. The light brush of his lips on hers aroused a soft moaning sigh from her, then his lips parted showing the gleam of strong teeth for a moment before he plunged downward and took her mouth, fiercely and hungrily, while his arms bound her tight enough to crush the breath from her.

Every emotion she had ever experienced clamoured and beat at her senses, sweeping her helplessly along towards surrender. Fear, hope, excitement and the need to conquer flowed from the hard, fierce mouth that possessed hers, until everything yielded to sheer irresistible desire—the desire to be one with the body and spirit that had kept her alive through all those hopeless days and nights.

The sudden shriek that snatched her from the brink struck like a physical blow, and just for a second Rowan felt she had actually stopped breathing. Rowa—a—a—a—n!'

René's howl of anguish shrilled like the cry of an animal in the hot still air, and sent a flight of parakeets skirling upward in a flutter of bright wings and shrill cries. Rowan closed her eyes and turned her head, seeking the haven she had so often sought in the past few days, pressing her brow to the hollow of James' shoulder.

She desired nothing more than to stay there, but James' big hands were on her arms and actually easing her away from him, so that she was bound to cry out against it. 'No, James!'

'It's a cry for help, sweetheart!' His voice had a harsh kind of urgency, suggesting just how near to oblivion he had been too, and he spoke close to her ear with his face buried in the silky mass of her hair that muffled his words. But Rowan didn't move, only clung more tightly to him. 'Rowan—girl, we can't ignore it!'

She nodded, but managed still to keep contact with the comforting warmth of tanned flesh, and she neither moved nor looked up. Eventually James slid a hand beneath her hair and curved the long fingers gently around her cheek,

lifting her head and looking down in to her face. He lightly
brushed his lips across her lowered lids.

'He has need of you, Rowan; you keep him sane.' It
was true, she knew it, but it did not make it any easier to
accept that James was so ready to recognise and allow it.

'I won't feel guilty, I *won't*, James! Even if he saw us!'

'You don't have to, sweetheart!' He regarded her with
the same bright burning look of untempered desire, and
she clung to the ecstasy of it for as long as she could. 'But
that's a man at the very end of his tether, and he needs
help; help we can't refuse him.'

'I know.'

He could have barely caught the whisper of it, but he
bent and kissed her forehead in that oddly paternal way he
had shown before, making her stir in instinctive protest,
lifting her head and shaking it. Even now, it seemed, he
could keep his head sufficiently to remember the bucket he
had so patiently filled from the stream, for he picked it
up with one hand while placing the other at Rowan's waist.

'Maggie will be scared stiff at him yelling like that.' His
long fingers squeezed slightly into her yielding flesh as if
to remind her. 'Come on, girl, we'd better go.'

Obediently Rowan went with him, but there was a gleam
of desperation in her eyes for the moment that had so
quickly been lost. And as James drew her with him across
the hot, unshaded clearing, her steps were stumbling and
clumsy because there were tears in her eyes.

René was sleeping. He looked pale and gaunt as he lay in
the same bunk bed that Rowan herself had occupied until recently, but he was resting at the moment, and so
could Rowan. The first aid box from the lifeboat had
proved a boon during the past few days, and it was a
sleeping draught of some kind that René had been given.
It was harmless enough, James had assured them, but
potent enough to ensure him a few hours' rest.

No one could really claim to be too surprised that René had finally cracked, for the signs had been there since they first landed on the island. He had never seemed able to come to terms with the alien environment as the rest of them had. Returning to the house with James, Rowan had found René weeping like a child, and the moment he saw her he clung to her hand and refused to let go, even when the draught took effect and he eventually went to sleep.

There seemed little likelihood of his being disturbed if she withdrew her hand now that he was asleep, but Rowan freed herself cautiously from his flaccid clasp nevertheless. Her attention was caught by voices from the next room and she immediately glanced across at the doorway, fearing the sound of them might rouse him. Paul and her grandmother only, she noticed, and since there was no indication that James was there he had probably gone off to search for salvage, as he had said he meant to.

René didn't stir, and she got up from the packing case that had served her as a seat, moving cautiously and tiptoeing across the room. It would have been an advantage had there been a door she could have closed behind her, as it was she glanced back at him and felt a curious mingling of pity and impatience, as well as a certain sympathy for herself as the unwitting cause of his breakdown. She had grown accustomed to his anger whenever he saw her and James together, but somehow the complete shattering of his self-control was unexpected as well as alarming.

Through in the main room, Paul Ordin and her grandmother looked up when she appeared, and anxiety was written deep on both their faces. Paul sat over in the far corner of the room, where the shadows were coolest, working on the radio that had so far proved much less of an advantage than they had hoped.

His thin dark face was tight with concentration and his head slightly bent and cocked to one side. He was a quiet, closed-in man since the death of his friends, and he said little, although Marguerite could sometimes draw him out. He had a determined fixation on putting life back into the unresponsive radio, but his smooth charm and ready wit had been lost with his companions in the fury of the storm.

Marguerite de Clare had never looked less like her former chic self than now, although she managed to retain her calm and also her cheerfulness for the most part. The dark silk dress she wore had once been elegant, but was limp and crumpled and no longer fitted, its sheen spoiled by water stains; and her once immaculate hair was pulled back from her face and gave her a much more severe look than normal. Her complexion, so carefully guarded through all her life, showed more lines than Rowan had ever seen, and her hands were rough and red, the nails broken and quite unlike the neat and polished ones that her regular manicurist knew.

Nevertheless she still smiled, even though it didn't quite reach her eyes, and Rowan felt a sudden surge of pride at the sheer undaunted courage of a woman who until now had never known any real discomfort in her life. Her smile had a weariness that tugged at Rowan's heart, but she still showed concern for the one member of their party who had admitted defeat and lost his nerve.

'Is René still sleeping?' she asked, and Rowan nodded.

She and Marguerite had a chair apiece, Paul making do with an upturned box, and just for a moment Rowan leaned back and closed her eyes. She hadn't realised quite how tired she was herself, although it was much more emotional tiredness than a physical one. The last few hours had been pretty wearing, and René's weeping, reproachful hysteria had come as a shock, following so soon on James' quite different assault on her emotions.

'I don't know what to do about him, Grand'mère.'

She hadn't opened her eyes when she spoke, but she could

feel her grandmother's gaze on her and imagine her faint frown as she mulled over her meaning .'You mean René?' she asked, and Rowan wondered just why she got the impression that she was playing for time.

The feeling was so strong that she opened her eyes and sat upright in her chair, looking across at Marguerite curiously. 'Of course I mean René,' she said, twining her own chafed hands restlessly in her lap. 'He—he's asked me to marry him, Grand'mère.'

Clearly it came as no surprise to Marguerite, although it was equally obvious that it gave her no pleasure either. 'So he told me,' she said, and Rowan again got the impression that she was being evasive.

'You mean he's spoken to you about it?' She disliked the idea, because involving her grandmother seemed to suggest René was trying to apply pressure by seeking her support. 'He shouldn't have done that, Grand'mère!'

'You think it doesn't concern me?'

'I think he's in too much of a hurry,' Rowan insisted. 'There's nothing at all between René and me, certainly nothing serious enough to tell you about. He shouldn't have mentioned it.'

'Perhaps not,' Marguerite allowed in a curiously absent tone of voice. 'At first I thought he was merely showing old-fashioned courtesy by asking my permission before he approached you, but then he told me that he'd already asked you and that you'd turned him down. I was thankful for that at least, child.'

'Don't you like René?'

'Yes, of course I like him,' said Marguerite, but something about her still made Rowan uneasy and she wished she knew what it was. 'He's handsome and charming and, in normal circumstances, very self-possessed. He's also wealthy, which is always an advantage, and he will make some lucky girl a very good husband.'

'But not me?'

'Not you, child.' Uneasy suspicions began to form in the recesses of Rowan's mind, and she tried to recognise them as she waited for further enlightenment. 'I told him that he was not for you because I knew it was the truth.'

There was a curious breathlessness about the confession that it took Rowan a second or two to begin to understand. Then her eyes widened and she stared in stunned silence for a moment, enlightenment coming with shattering suddenness. 'You—you didn't give him any reason, did you, Grand'mère?'

Clearly she had, for the telling was not easy and Marguerite de Clare had never seemed so much at a loss as she did at that moment. 'He came and asked for my consent to your marriage; he said that he loved you and he was sure that you loved him. He told me that he had asked you to marry him, and although you'd said no, he was sure he could bring you round once you were away from James' influence.' Rowan said nothing, but sat with her hands tightly folded together and her eyes downcast. 'I told him,' Marguerite went on, 'I told him that there was very little chance for him in my opinion, because you were in love with James and James with you.'

'Oh no!'

Her whispered plea brought Marguerite's eyes up too, and Rowan saw the tears that shimmered in them, clouding their darkness and bringing a helpless look that was too alien to be easily acceptable. Her voice too lacked its firm control and emerged as a hoarse whisper that was barely recognisable.

'If only I'd realised, Rowan!' She clasped her hands tightly to stop them trembling, but Rowan suspected that talking about it came as a relief. 'I didn't realise how close to breaking point he was, or what it was that kept him going. When I told him, I thought—I thought for a moment that he was going to kill me. I have never seen such a look in a man's eyes before, and something about him must have struck Paul, although he hadn't heard any of what was said. I believe René would have struck me if Paul hadn't come across; as it was, he stood there with tears pouring down his face and crying like a child, until he turned away suddenly and went into the bedroom. It was only a second or two afterwards that——'

Rowan knew exactly what had happened after that. James had kissed her; right out there in full view of the broken bedroom window, and she had been in a seventh heaven of delight, right in his arms, with his mouth and his hard, virile body chasing away the frustrations and discomforts of that hateful island, pushing back the possibility of their never being found. Then René had called out in anguish and snatched her back from the brink of sweet oblivion.

'I heard him,' she whispered, covering her face with a hand for a moment. 'James and I were in the clearing.'

'Together?' Rowan knew exactly what she meant by that, and she nodded. 'Oh, poor, poor René!'

The sound of that cry seared her nerves again in recollection, and Rowan shuddered. 'It was like—like the cry of an animal,' she said huskily. 'I've never heard anything so—soul-destroying, it was awful!'

It was appalling too to face the fact that until they were discovered and taken off that vicious, swamp-ridden island, she was bound to René by a bond tighter than any he had tried to bind her with before. For almost certainly James would see it as the right thing to do, he might even insist that she play a game of make-believe with René to preserve his sanity.

At the thought of it tears streamed down her cheeks and she was unaware of it until the light slow fall of them on to her clasped hands brought the realisation that she was crying. In a moment Marguerite had left her chair and was standing beside her, drawing her close and soothing and stroking her head until her face was half hidden in the rumpled fullness of her skirt.

'Oh, my darling child, what can I do to help you? I feel so helpless, so—responsible.'

'No, no, I won't have that!' Rowan denied it swiftly and urgently, for she could not bear the thought of Marguerite carrying the blame for what had happened. 'It was no more your fault than anyone else's, Grand'mère, we all knew René was on the brink of hysteria—I heard it the very first night when he came for me, to my cabin. But until we get away from this—this awful place, we can't do anything about anything. It's just a hopeless muddle and I can't see an end in sight at the moment.'

'James does love you?' Even now Marguerite could give importance to romance as easily as to other matters, but it wasn't a question that Rowan could answer with any certainty. She wished she could.

'James likes kissing girls,' she said after a moment or two, and made an attempt to smile, though not a very successful one. 'I don't know that it's love, although it's very romantic and exciting, and I have to confess that I like being kissed by James, partly because it helps me forget where we are and how hopeless and miserable it all is.' She brushed a hand across her eyes and rubbed away the tears, then looked up at her grandmother. 'He and René both play the field, you know,' she told her, being deliberately casual. 'They indulge in affairs as often as they change their shirts, it seems to me, so I'd be rather silly to take either of them very seriously.'

'Not even René?' Marguerite asked, and it was clear that her own part in René's breakdown still worried her.

Rowan sighed and glanced briefly across to the corner where Paul was bent over the radio, and she shook her head. 'I suppose that for the moment I'll have to take René seriously,' she allowed, and tried not to let it be seen how she felt. 'I imagine James will be a lot more reserved too, for fear of making matters worse.'

'And that concerns you?' Marguerite suggested softly.

It wasn't easy to find an answer that would not betray far too much, and Rowan did not look at her when she eventually found the words. 'It will mean I'll have to pretend something I don't feel,' she replied cautiously. 'I—like James; he's been very good to me and good *for* me. I've relied on him an awful lot and I don't think I can suddenly pretend I don't need him—need his help and encouragement any less, not even to placate René.'

'My poor baby!'

Marguerite pulled her head towards her, clasping it to her firm bosom, crooning in sympathy, just as she had so often done when Rowan was a child. And just for a moment Rowan allowed herself the luxury of relaxing completely, as if there was no one else but the two of them in the whole world.

In the background a harsh crackling noise prickled the uneasy quiet, and Paul Ordin murmured something half under his breath, but neither of the women stirred out of their own little cocoon of misery for the moment. Then it happened again; the sharp crackle penetrated Rowan's reluctant consciousness, and a further short, soft exclamation from Paul made her lift her head and try to peer around her grandmother at him.

Marguerite herself turned right around and faced him, and her hands were tightly clenched at her sides, her body quivering with tension as she held herself firmly in control. 'What is it, *mon cher*?' she asked, and Paul Ordin raised his thin dark face for a moment and stared blankly.

Then the radio crackled once more and a distant voice, harsh and distorted, babbled briefly in the silent room. 'It's working, *madame*!' He stared at the crackling, screeching radio as if it was some kind of miracle. 'The radio's working, it's *working*!'

Marguerite grasped the back of Rowan's chair with one hand, and just briefly Rowan saw her sway. But her re-

covery was swift, and she turned and looked down at
Rowan with eyes that brimmed tears, her face flushed
pink like that of a young girl. Reaching for Rowan's hands
she squeezed them hard, and all the agony of the past few
days was in the dark anxious eyes that watched the man in
the corner shadows.

'Be sure, *mon cher*,' she told Paul in a throaty whisper of
sound. 'Be very sure, my dear, dear Paul.'

The radio answered for itself, spattering the air with
sounds, faint and harsh, but sounds of the outside world
they had been cut off from for so long. 'I'm sure, *madame*,'
Paul told her, and his haggard dark face was illumined by a
look of ecstasy. 'It has happened, it's working; listen for
yourself, it's working!'

Tears rolled down his face and he looked from one to
the other of them as if he sought their assurance that he
was not merely suffering from a delusion. Marguerite
crossed the room to him and clasped him in her arms,
cradling him like a child and murmuring congratulations
and assurances.

'You have worked a miracle, *mon cher*, a miracle! Oh,
but you are so clever!' She kissed him soundly on his
mouth and Paul laughed in sheer exuberance.

Rowan too kissed him, and in her case he put his arms
around her and made the salute last much longer, but
once again he laughed when he let her go. It was hard to
remember René, still and quiet in a drugged sleep, when
there was suddenly so much to hope for, but Rowan put a
finger to her lips when the excited chatter grew in volume,
and Marguerite took her meaning, shrugging herself to
silence and shaking a warning head at Paul.

'We won't wake René yet,' she decreed. Her voice was
kept low so as not to wake him, but it shivered still with
the excitement that possessed them all and her eyes
gleamed like jet when she turned to Rowan and clasped
her hand tightly. 'But go and tell James! Go, child, go

and find him and tell him!' Rowan needed no second bidding. She darted across the room and was almost through the open doorway when Marguerite called after her. 'And it is permitted that you kiss him when you give him the news, *chérie*—who could object at such a time?'

Rowan laughed and it was like being released from imprisonment, for it seemed such a very long time since she had laughed like that. She was still smiling as she ran round the hut, making for the narrow strip of jungle that separated them from the ocean, for her feet felt as light as her head and barely seemed to touch the ground.

The tangle of vegetation obliged her to slow down, but she was already glowing and moist with the heat, and her breath was drawn in short hard gasps as she followed James' path to the shore. Parakeets soared upward in a bright cloud of wings, scolding loudly, and must have inevitably given James warning of her coming. Her own unsuspected weakness slowed her to the point when she fumed with impatience, but tearing aside the vines that impeded her progress, she smiled suddenly when she caught a glimpse of ocean through the trees and of a tawny-headed man kneeling on the sand at the edge of the trees.

At the sight of him she felt as if her heart would stop, but then the fact of his kneeling took on significance suddenly and she slowed her approach almost to a standstill, making her much more cautious than she had planned to be. Something about the scene before her touched her overheated body with the chill of ice and added fear to the sensations that already pulsed wildly through her. It was suddenly identifying for what it was, the mound of sand beside which he knelt, that pulled her up short at the very moment when she would have called out to him. For the significance of its length and shape was unmistakable, and drew a long shuddering sigh from her.

Standing some distance from the spot where he knelt,

Rowan watched him get slowly to his feet and brush down his slacks with such an air of detachment it was obvious he did it automatically. He held a length of driftwood in one hand that had obviously served as a shovel, and it was when he flung it away from him that he noticed Rowan. Hovering uncertainly at the edge of the trees, her emotions were torn two ways, between the excitement she had felt when she came to find him, and the sadness of this latest occurrence, and she was unsure how to approach him.

'Rowan!'

The problem was solved when James held out a hand as he started across towards her, but it seemed so incredibly hard to believe that he was actually seeking her sympathy and comfort that just for a second she hesitated. It was doubtful if he had time to notice her hesitation, for she realised his need suddenly and jerked into action; running swiftly along the ridge of trees to meet him, breathless and anxious as he clasped her hand tightly in his.

He didn't take her in his arms as she half expected him to do, but simply held her hand while they walked along together, and he glanced back only briefly over his shoulder. Still tense and uncertain what to say, Rowan too glanced uneasily in the same direction, and she had to moisten her dry lips with the tip of her tongue before she could speak.

'Who—who is it?' she whispered.

'Steven.'

There was so much more than mere regret in his voice that she felt her heart thud urgently in pity, and her breath caught momentarily in her throat at the realisation that something that had until then been an unconfirmed fear was now a stark reality.

She remembered a small man, scarcely taller than herself and with wispy sandy hair, who was invariably bright and cheerful; his face as wrinkled as a prune and weathered to a dark mahogany. Somehow it was much harder to take the second time of hearing, and the loss seemed much greater with that small silent mound of sand down there.

'I'm—I'm sory, James.'

What else could she say to him? He had known both Bill and Steven for years and their loss must inevitably mean much more to him, but she could understand his blank look of shock and she wished there was something she could do to help him.

'I was scavenging on the beach.' He seemed to want to talk about it, and perhaps, she thought, that was the best thing. 'I found nothing of any use and I was about to give up, then——' The curiously flat voice was silenced for a moment and Rowan squeezed hard on the fingers that held hers. 'He was on the beach at the far side of the bay and I didn't realise at first, I thought——' He shook his head. 'I didn't find Bill, but the tides could vary and he could be somewhere—anywhere. At the moment I just haven't the heart to go and look.'

'Paul might go,' she ventured, and James shook his head.

'He's been through enough and he and Bill were very good friends. He was shattered at losing them both; you saw him.'

He held her hand so tightly that it hurt, but Rowan could guess that the hurt he was feeling was far worse and she suffered it uncomplainingly. So far they hadn't turned inland, but were walking parallel with the ocean, a slow pace that at times almost stopped altogether, and it was still possible to glance back and see that telltale mound. Rowan wished it wasn't, because it brought home to her just how vulnerable they all were in this small hostile world of sun and sea.

'There was nothing else I could do, Rowan, except—what I did.' James' voice snatched her back swiftly to immediate matters, and she looked up at his drawn, cold face. 'Though God knows—just a heap of sand——'

'You couldn't have done more,' she assured him quickly,

and again pressed her own slim fingers into his. 'You did all you could, James.'

A fallen tree lay beside their path, and James glanced across at it. All but its dead root was buried in the encroaching sand, and its trunk was scarred by storm winds; another victim of the fury the tropics were capable of. To Rowan it was much too near the reminder of old Steven, but James sat down on it as if he was suddenly too tired to walk any further. Hands pressed over his face, muffled his words as well as hid his expression, but it was enough that the deep, firm voice had never before sounded so dispirited.

'I've known him all my life and I can't believe he's gone.' He lifted his head, but he gazed at the ocean rather than look at her, and he spoke as if to himself, Rowan thought. 'Long before I had the *Belle* he did odd jobs around the kitchens, which was a wicked waste because he was a damned good cook. I remember when he asked me to take him on, when I first got the *Belle*, he wanted to come with me as cook, and I laughed.' He brushed his hands through his hair in a gesture of despair gazing unseeingly at the ocean. 'I shouldn't have laughed, because he proved how good he was by sneaking stuff from the kitchen and cooking up things he knew I liked! In the end I took him on as cook, just for his cheek, and I was never sorry I did—until now.'

Again he glanced at the pile of shimmering white sand, then bowed his head to his hands again, his broad shoulders dropped despondently. To Rowan his vulnerability was unexpected and very touching, and the glad news about the radio that she had come to bring him was completely forgotten in her desire to comfort him as he had so often comforted her.

Moving closer to him, she put her hands either side of his head and drew him to her until his face was laid comfortingly on her breast, then she hugged him close, her fingers stroking and soothing and infinitely gentle. 'Oh, Jamie, Jamie!' His childhood name seemed somehow appropriate at such a moment, and James made no objection to it, but pressed closer and closed his eyes. 'Oh, my dear, I'm so sorry.' Her whisper stirred his thick tawny hair and she laid her face on it for a moment before pressing her lips to his forehead.

Perhaps at first it had been very like comforting a child, but there was nothing childlike about the strong arms that bound her tight to him, or in the touch of the smooth naked chest that pressed warmly to her own body. And it was almost as if their combined senses reacted in unison when her hands moved downward to the nape of his neck and curled tightly into the thick hair, and his head turned slightly, bringing his lips to the vee of soft flesh where her shirt opened.

'Rowan!'

He whispered her name hoarsely and pulled her down to him, crushing her in his arms and burying his face in the hot, sweet softness of her neck. Rowan responded willingly and lifted her arms to clasp them around his neck, her body shivering with the desire to be still closer to him, and it was only when he groaned aloud as he took her mouth that she realised his passion in this instance was partly a salve for his despair.

'James!' The moment he released her mouth she turned her face to the familiar hollow of his shoulder and clung to him tightly, and once more he buried his face in the softness of her hair. 'James, I came——' She sought blindly through the chaos of her emotions, trying to find the reason she'd had for coming to look for him, but it wasn't until James himself voiced his own fervent wishes that she remembered.

'Oh God, if only we could get away from this damned place!' he murmured harshly; and in defiance of her

clamorous senses, Rowan lifted her head and eased herself
away from him just slightly.

'That was what I came to tell you,' she said in a quiet
voice, and touched a finger lightly to the lowered tip of one
brow when he frowned. 'Paul's got the radio going—it's
working, James, I heard it!'

'Are you——' He stared at her for a moment almost as
if he was afraid to believe it. 'Rowan, sweetheart, say that
again.'

Rowan lifted her face to him, her eyes glowing and her
heart thudding in wild response to the steady hard beat
of his. 'I heard it before I came to look for you,' she assured
him, and James flung back his great leonine head and yelled
his exultation to the skies, then kissed her so long and so
hard that she clung to him breathlessly.

'It works!' He repeated the words as if they were a kind
of prayer, then once more buried his face in the softness of
her hair. 'Oh, sweetheart, you don't know how often I've
thought of us stuck here on this damned island until——'
Raising his head he looked beyond her to the solitary
mound at the edge of the trees, then he shook his head.
'The old boy would have been the first to wish us luck,'
he said. 'Even though he didn't make it himself.'

'I'm certain he would.' She gave a brief backward glance,
then got to her feet when James did, and followed him as
he turned inland, and she wasn't quite sure what made
her mention René at that particular moment. 'We haven't
broken the news to René yet, James,' she told him. 'He
was still asleep and we thought it best not to wake him;
it's better that he sleeps as long as possible.'

James said nothing, but he gave her a long hard look
before he turned to lead the way back, and not for the first
time Rowan found herself wishing she knew what was
going on behind those very disturbing blue eyes. She had
learned a great deal about James since they landed in their

present predicament, but she was convinced that he was a very complex man.

There were a great many other things still to be learned about him, she felt sure, and she had an insatiable desire to know all there was to know about him. Her fear now was that with rescue ever nearer she might not have time to find out all she wanted to know.

CHAPTER EIGHT

IT seemed the most awful anti-climax when, having got the radio working, their repeated calls brought no response. The possibility of not being able to raise immediate help had not even occurred to Rowan, and her initial elation had given way to a slightly edgy anxiety that was shared to some degree by the rest of the party.

René's attitude did nothing to make things easier for Rowan either, for his moods alternated between wild excitement at the prospect of being rescued and the gloomy conviction that they never would be. Although Paul and Marguerite had visited that solitary grave on the seashore, no one had so far said anything to René about it, and it was by common consent that he was let off doing any of the chores.

It was hard to concentrate on the simple everyday needs like collecting food and eating meals, when at any moment the radio might crackle out a promise of rescue, and yet activity was the best antidote for the interminable waiting. Paul was poised over the radio as he had been for most of the night, and James was foraging for their next meal, while Marguerite kept the fire burning that was their only means of cooking and heating water.

Rowan was yet again keeping René company. He was

possessive and demanding and seemed never to recognise
her need to be free of him occasionally, and yet it was difficult to condemn him too harshly for he had not come
through their ordeal nearly so well as even Rowan had. He
looked drawn and pale-faced and Rowan felt sorry for him,
but pity was all she felt. She recognised that fact quite
clearly at last, but in the present situation did not quite
know what to do about it.

They sat on the balcony in the two chairs brought out
from the house and set close together at René's instigation.
Thus it was easy for him to reach for her hand and hold it
for a minute before raising it to his lips and kissing her
fingers. *'Chérie!'* He was in one of his optimistic moods
and he whispered softly and with the fervour of a lover.
Yet for all that Rowan got the feeling that she was as
much a lifeline to which he clung, as she was a paramour.
'Soon now,' he promised, and when she looked at him he
smiled.

'It can't be long, surely,' she agreed, as much to assure
herself as René. 'Someone must pick up our signal soon
I should think.'

'And then we'll go home.' René spread out her slim
fingers with his own, then kissed them one by one. When
he glanced up there was a deep glowing fervour in his eyes
that made her shudder because she felt in some way
trapped. 'And then we'll begin to live, eh, *ma chérie?* No
more jungle, no more heat and mud and that eternal fruit
we're expected to eat day after day! Ugh—God in heaven,
I never want to see another orange or banana as long as I
live!'

It was inevitable that Rowan should react defensively;
she invariably did when James' care of them was criticised,
however indirectly, and she spoke up quickly. 'Don't be so
disparaging about it, René! At least you've had something
to eat, *and* without the effort of going foraging for it! If
it wasn't for the oranges and bananas and things that you

complain you're so sick of, you'd have been dead long since, we all would! We owe our lives to whatever James and Paul can find for us, and don't you forget it!'

'I'm never likely to be given the chance to!' René replied sharply, and his hand squeezed her bruisingly hard for a moment as if in reprimand. It was, Rowan mused, a gesture typical of René that he blamed her for reminding him. 'However grateful I am for small mercies,' he went on, 'I still don't want to see fruit again for a very long time once we get back to civilisation.' His charm returned, as smoothly as if it had never momentarily slipped, and he was smiling again. 'Anyway, my darling, the moment we get back I promise you the most huge and delicious meal you've ever eaten.' Getting up out of his chair, he was only slightly clumsy on the almost healed ankle, and he offered her his hands, gazing at her with bright luminous eyes. 'Afterwards—Ah, *mignonne*!'

He pulled her slowly to her feet, but Rowan was reluctant to leave her chair, for she guessed what would inevitably follow, and she kept distance between them for as long as possible. Not for long, however, for he drew her into his arms and she could feel his eyes on her face, watching her as he always seemed to now. His hands slid around her, coaxing, seeking her response, and it took all the control that Rowan was capable of not to push him away.

Instead she merely stood passive and unresponsive in his arms, with her head bent and her eyes downcast. She couldn't bear to think that James would expect her to go to any length to keep René from again sinking into that awful state of despair, and she steeled herself against the touch of René's body as he pulled her closer. She felt none of the wild excitement that being close to James gave her, and her senses clamoured against the growing intimacy of his embrace.

His lips brushed her neck, murmuring incomprehensible words all the time, then travelled upward to her jaw and the

soft, clear line of her cheek, to her mouth. His voice was
low and seductive and his breath warm on her lips, but her
heart responded only with near panic, and thudded hard
under René's caressing fingers, as if at betrayal.

'Lovely Rowan,' he breathed, teasing her lips with his.
'My lovely, adorable Rowan, you *do* love me, don't you?'
He kissed her lightly without waiting for the reply that she
would have found impossible to form honestly. His kiss
became more forceful, and he seemed not to notice how
unresponsive she was; and when he released her mouth
and laughed, it had a ring of triumph. 'I knew you loved
me, even James is ready to acknowledge it now!' He spoke
as if he had no doubt at all that she shared his pleasure. 'He
hasn't bothered you since—that day, has he?'

He shied away from the subject of his breakdown, and
Rowan could understand how he felt about it. The experience must have been doubly harrowing for him, brief as
it was, and she could guess he preferred to push it to the
back of his mind. But he knew nothing about those few
moments with James, just after he had buried Steven, or
he would have been much less complacent.

She wondered if he would even be touched at all if he
knew about the silent mound of sand on the beach, and
doubted it very much. It was becoming increasingly evident
that René's interest was limited to his own comfort and
well-being, and it startled her to realise how close she was
to actively disliking him—something she would never have
believed possible during those lazy, luxurious weeks aboard
the yacht.

'I knew he'd eventually realise the way things stood,'
René went on confidently. 'He just had to try and take you
away from me because he doesn't like losing!'

'Do *you*?'

Her swift retort obviously took him by surprise and he
looked at her curiously for a second or two. 'No, of course
I don't, darling,' he told her, and smiled. 'But I haven't
lost in the final reckoning, have I? When we get back to

normal and you don't have to depend on him for your food and his knowledge of how to survive in a jungle, then you'll see him as just as crude and uncultured as you first thought him. You were much more astute than I was in that instance, my love, but I see him now as you did right from the beginning.'

'René——'

'Oh, when I think of it!' He heaved a sigh of anticipation while Rowan ruefully saw her earlier opinions coming home to roost and wondered how she could have been so blind. 'Just think, darling, James will disappear back to his barbaric Highlands, and you and I will be safe in *la belle France* with no one to come between us. Oh, I've so often dreamed about it since we landed on this ghastly place, my sweet! I swear I'll never set foot on another boat as long as I live, and especially not one captained by James Fraser!'

'Oh, for heaven's sake, stop it!'

René stared at her in astonishment when she struggled free of his embrace and turned from him sharply. She was shaking in every limb and trying hard not to let him see how close to tears she was. It was a curious sensation, an alarming one, imagining a situation where she would never see James again, and she couldn't pretend to enjoy the prospect as René obviously expected her to. Whether or not he became upset again, she couldn't let the charade go on.

'My darling!'

'No, I'm *not* your darling!'

When he placed a tentative hand on her shoulder and tried to turn her to face him again, she shrugged away from him and something seemed to hover in the air between them other than the steamy jungle heat. Her heart was thudding, making her breathless, and she turned swiftly and was half-way across the clearing before René recovered sufficiently to call after her.

'Rowan, what's wrong? Rowan, *chérie*!'

But Rowan kept going, not consciously going in any particular direction but instinctively following a trail that was now well marked by James and Paul on their frequent forays for food. She didn't choose her path, it was chosen for her by the broken trees and vines that bored a passage into the dark depths of the undergrowth. But before long she began to realise that the hot, steaming marsh and sunless heat revived certain memories.

It was hard to believe that there could be any good ones among them, and yet she could remember things that had been actually pleasurable if she thought back. Pushing aside a broken vine that hung across her path, she recalled some of them. Things like the constant reassurance of James' company, and the very special feeling of being in his arms, for whatever reason. Most of all the times he had kissed her, though they had been few enough. No amount of applied common sense could make her believe that his kisses had always been merely to comfort her, and the remembered thrill of his strength and passion surged through her like a rekindled flame.

Something she heard just ahead of her made her stop for a moment and listen, for James was out foraging somewhere, and it was more than likely him she had heard. The rustle of movement among the brush sent birds into panic flight, and her own heart was thudding hard as she felt that now familiar tightening sensation in her stomach that anticipated his coming. With the idea of surprising him she pressed on along the well marked trail, lifting an arm to sweep aside yet another hanging vine from her path.

Only in this instance the vine moved of its own accord in the second that she reached out to brush it away, looping itself in yet another turn over the branch it dangled from, and Rowan screamed. She had a horror of reptiles and during their search for her grandmother she had more than once experienced a nasty moment, although never at such close quarters as this.

Her scream had been purely an instinctive reaction, and so also was her sudden flight. She turned, giving the apparently passive reptile a brief horrified glance over her shoulder as she dashed back through the undergrowth, heedless now of the direction she took. Stumbling and tripping over roots and slipping on the marshy ground, she broke new ground without even realising it in her haste to get away, and stopped only when she was too limp to run any more.

It was too soon after the debilitating bout of heat-stroke for such exertion and she clung to the support of a tree breathing hard and painfully. Her head was pounding and her legs almost too weak to support her as she stood with her eyes closed and tried to gather her elusive courage, hearing nothing for a moment but the thudding beat of her own heart.

'Rowan!' The cry had a flat, muffled sound coming through the thick undergrowth. But Rowan would have known James' voice anywhere, and she tried to summon breath enough to answer, listening in the meantime to the crack of branches and rustling whish of leaves as he forced his way towards her. 'Rowan, where are you, girl?' A heavy body came crashing through the virgin path she had broken, and she managed to raise her voice at last.

'James—over here!'

His sense of direction must have been pretty good, for he found her almost at once and seemed almost surprised when she shook her head to deny any cause for anxiety, and even managed a ghost of a smile. He was frowning, inevitably, his light brows drawn into thunderous condemnation as he came thrusting through the tangle of brush to her, and his first words were not altogether encouraging.

'What's the kerfuffle? What the devil are you doing out here, you daft wee creature?'

'I'm— all right.'

'I can see that!' Nevertheless he put a hand to her brow and her senses made the inevitable response to his touch, bringing more colour to her already flushed cheeks. Finding nothing seriously amiss, he apparently felt entitled to lay down the law on the subject of not doing as he had instructed. 'I told you to stay in the cool and not to exert yourself until you're stronger,' he reminded her firmly. 'What's the idea of running around out here in the heat and getting yourself into a sweat that we'll have to remedy if you're not to go down ill again? Why didn't you stay put?'

'Oh, stop nagging me, James!'

When she remembered the reason for her walking off and leaving René, his condemnation seemed doubly unfair, although she had no intention of letting him know how she had championed him. But it was all a bit too much and reaction was setting in. She was still shattered from her close encounter with the snake, and now to top it all James was bullying her instead of being gentle and comforting.

Her lower lip thrust out in reproach and although she wasn't actually crying, the threat of tears shimmered in her eyes and gave them a misty grey look that was infinitely appealing.

'I didn't know I *was* nagging you,' James told her, and a very faint smile touched his mouth with the more familiar humour. 'But I'll stop pointing out what a daft wee nut you are, if you give me a good reason for being out here instead of taking it easy.' A glimmer of anticipation gleamed in his eyes for a moment. 'Paul hasn't managed to raise somebody at last, has he? Is that what you came to tell me?'

If only she could have told him it was for that reason she came to look for him, but she shook her head reluctantly and lowered her gaze rather than see the look in his eyes and the resigned shrug of his shoulders. 'No, there's still nothing; I wish I could say there was, James.'

'So do I,' James said ruefully. 'So—give me a good reason for being out here and for screaming your head off and scaring me out of ten years' growth.'

'I'm sorry.' He dismissed the apology with an impatient hand, and waited for enlightenment. 'I saw a snake.'

One brow arched slightly, and he regarded her for a moment in silence. 'It didn't harm you?'

'No.'

'You've seen enough snakes since we got here,' he reminded her, 'and you've never screamed your head off about it before.'

Rowan shrugged uneasily. She wished he would stop being so determinedly practical and take her in his arms, and when he took a sudden step nearer it was almost as if he meant to do as she hoped. He brought that alarmingly affecting aura of masculinity much too close for comfort, but he still didn't touch her. Instead his eyes searched her with frank explicitness; first her face and then her body, barely covered by the remnant of her own cotton skirt and his shirt.

'Why, Rowan?' he asked softly, and the nearness of him played with her senses like a cat with a mouse.

'I was scared stiff,' she told him. 'You know how terrified I am of snakes.'

It was said reproachfully and with a slight thrust of her lip, while she looked up at him through the thick darkness of her lashes. 'And you think I'm a callous brute for not being more sympathetic, is that it?' James guessed. His light blue eyes smiled at her in that warm and secret way he had. 'Poor wee Rowan!'

She hastily looked away, because she had the feeling suddenly that she was betraying far more than she dared do at this moment. 'You're not usually so—stand-offish,' she told him, and flicked him another swift upward glance when he laughed shortly.

'So that's why you screamed; because you knew I was about somewhere,' he said, and Rowan caught her breath.

'Of course it wasn't!' She denied it hastily but wondered why she felt out of her depth with him for the first time. 'The wretched thing was hanging from a branch right in front of me, and you know how I feel about snakes! You know perfectly well, James!'

He was too close and not close enough, and Rowan's senses were in confusion. Until that moment she had been certain that her scream had been prompted purely and simply by the reptile's sudden and unexpected proximity. Now she had to ask herself whether or not she would have given voice quite so loudly if she hadn't known that James was in the vicinity, and it was a disconcerting thought.

James had always had the ability to arouse certain responses in her, but just at the moment she felt she had never been in more need of him. If she just reached out a hand she could touch him; she could smooth her fingers over the lean tanned body that had become leaner and more tanned in the past days, like the rest of them. But he still did not touch her, and she did not know what to make of his abstention.

'So that accounts for the scream,' he said, and the softly rolling r's teased her senses further. 'But I still don't know what brought you out here if it wasn't to tell me that we've made contact with a possible rescuer.'

His eyes once more slid over her face in that lazy but explicit study that was so disturbing. 'I had a—sort of argument with René,' she said, and James raised his eyes to heaven.

'Oh, great, that should ensure another scene for certain!'

'Don't, please don't, James!' Her protest was swift and defensive, for she couldn't face it if he insisted she carried on with that pretence with René. 'I can't do it any longer!' There was a note of desperation in her voice that she was unaware of at the moment. 'I can't pretend to be in love with him when I'm not, and—and you're cruel to expect me to! I don't love him, James, and I can't pretend I do—I don't *want* to pretend I do! René doesn't really love me, not—not in that way.'

'Mebbe not.' The admission surprised her and she looked up to see him smiling in that slow and oddly touching way of his. 'But he's dependent on you, Rowan, and needing someone in that way *is* a kind of loving, isn't it?'

'I—I don't know.'

Rowan wasn't ready to admit it, for she had already quite made up her mind that she loved James as she had never loved anyone in her life before, and he was putting a doubt into her mind. He knew how she felt, she was almost sure of it, for she had done little to conceal it during the past few minutes, and yet he was offering her a reason for a different kind of loving. It wasn't the time for coyness or pretence, and when she looked up at him her eyes were bright with all the love and warmth she felt just being with him.

'But it isn't like that with me,' she insisted, as if he had made a straightforward suggestion that it was, and her voice was very small and unsteady. 'It isn't like that, James.'

He made contact at last, reaching out a hand to lightly touch her cheek and to scoop up a big rolling tear with a forefinger, and the surge of emotion that he brought with that slight contact caught at her breath. 'Isn't it?' he murmured, and bent to kiss her eyes, pressing his lips to her half-closed lids and wet lashes. 'You've become too dependent on me, Rowan. I don't propose making a catalogue of my virtues, but I know from what Maggie's told me that you feel you owe me your life, for one thing, and that isn't the state of mind to decide whether or not you're in love.'

'But James——'

He slid a hand beneath her chin and his thumb pressed over her lips and silenced her, then moved slowly and caressingly back and forth when she pursed her lips to its touch. 'We'll all be going home soon, time enough when you're back in your own environment to commit yourself.'

'Don't you care?'

Her voice and her eyes reproached him, for she had not until that moment doubted his caring as she did. James smiled faintly and leaned to kiss her soft and very vulnerable mouth, a lingering kiss that she sought to prolong even more. 'I'm not going to commit myself either. Oh, I know how I feel,' he added quickly when he saw the question looming. 'But it's much better that you take a second look when you get home among all your familiar places and people.'

'There isn't anyone!'

She declared it quickly, and again he bent and kissed her lips, very lightly this time. 'Then it should be easier to think straight,' he told her.

The full meaning of going home hadn't really registered with her until then and she looked up at him anxiously. 'You'll be going back to Scotland?' she guessed, and somehow managed to make it sound like an accusation.

'Where else, girl?' James asked, and passed his thumb caressingly over her lips again. 'It's my home, where else would I go?'

Never before had the two countries seemed so far apart, and Rowan had never before felt so completely and utterly unhappy. She felt vulnerable too, because with just one wrong word James could shatter her whole world, and she couldn't help recalling how she had told her grandmother that both he and René liked to play the field. Perhaps it was James' way of letting her down lightly, by suggesting that it was she who needed to make quite sure how she felt. At the thought of that being true tears streamed down her cheeks and she stood with closed eyes, her hair drifting forward to help hide the fact that she was crying and could do nothing about it.

'Oh, don't cry, sweetheart, please! Please don't cry!' James reached out for her and took her in his arms, and to Rowan it was like going home. She turned her face into his shoulder and yielded herself to the strength and comfort of his arms, while one big hand stroked over her hair and the other curved caressingly under the soft swell of her breast as he held her so tightly she could scarcely breathe. 'You'll be home again soon, and—well, things could look very different from a distance.'

'They won't, I know they won't!'

Her voice was muffled but adamant, and she heard James' light, rueful laughter as from a distance and half smothered in her hair. 'If you say so, little one,' he agreed obligingly, and the suspicion of paternalism in his voice was something she had noted on other occasions but never resented quite as much as she did now.

Looking up, she frowned at him, refusing to be soothed. 'I wish you wouldn't talk to me as if I was a baby,' she told him in shaky tones. 'I'm twenty-two, James, not two, and I don't like being pacified like a babe in arms!'

He looked down at her flushed face and laughter lurked in his eyes with a gleam of challenge. 'That's *just* what you are! And I can give you ten years in age and a hell of a lot more in experience, my girl, so don't try picking a fight with me!' Something about him held her silent when she would have objected, and she too looked vaguely in the direction of a half-heard sound, listening for it to be repeated. 'Did you hear it too?' James asked, and she nodded.

'René,' she guessed, and James eased her away, though not from any fear of René's sudden appearance, she felt sure.

James turned aside, then gave her a brief and oddly rueful smile. 'News?' he speculated, then went striding off away from her, leaving her to follow in his wake, her heart suddenly beating wildly and urgently with a tumult of emotions.

Hampered by an injured ankle, René hadn't made a lot of progress, but James was quicker, swift and sure over now almost familiar ground, and Rowan scrambled after him, drawn by the same sense of anticipation that gave a jerky impatience to his long step. It was James who called out to him when he again caught the sound of his name just ahead.

'Here, René, I'm on my way!'

'Thank God!' René remarked thankfully. 'It's murder trying to walk with this blasted ankle. Paul's got a——' He broke off for only a second when Rowan came close on James' heels, and his expression barely changed, almost as if he expected to see them together. 'There's a South American merchantman in the vicinity and they're coming to pick us up! They'll be here in about three or four hours!'

James murmured something that neither of them quite caught, but his tawny, leonine head was clasped in his hands briefly and Rowan had to hold herself tightly in check so that she did not run to him and clasp her arms around him. His ice-blue eyes turned on her and he smiled, a smile that was somehow touching and very vulnerable.

'It'll not be long now, sweetheart,' he told her, 'and you'll be home and dry. We all shall.'

René darted a swift glance between them, and it was almost as if he suspected that almost-quarrel back there when he flung an arm around her and hugged her close, kissing her cheek, because Rowan very carefully turned her mouth from him. '*La belle France, ma chérie,*' he murmured, and still with an arm around her, turned her in the direction of the hut. 'I shall be treating you to that huge meal very soon now, darling, eh?'

James was ahead of them, and it was impossible to tell what he was thinking about René's plans, if indeed he was thinking of anything but their imminent rescue. But whether or not he could hear their conversation or was interested in it, Rowan was thinking of other things than having dinner with René, and she slipped from his embrace suddenly and ran on ahead in search of her grandmother.

Marguerite was outside on the balcony and she was smiling, a broad beaming smile as she held out her arms. It was some distance across the clearing and Rowan was still running, until James' voice came after her, quiet but commanding. 'Slow down, you daft wee creature, or you'll be flat on your back and swathed in wet sheets again!'

Her first instinct was to defy him, but even before he had finished admonishing her, she had slowed to a more sedate pace, and she stuck her chin in the air in defiance of her grandmother's approving nod. 'A bossy Leo man!' she murmured under her breath, but smiled for all that.

The South American merchantman stood off from the island, looking smaller somehow than Rowan expected, but like the rest of them, she kept her eyes mainly on the longboat that was making its way laboriously towards them through the heavy sea. Her heart was thudding hard and her head was buzzing with a myriad thoughts and impressions.

She was glad to be going, of course she was, but there was nevertheless a certain feeling of nostalgia as she stood for the last time on the tiny beach where she had walked with James, and been kissed in a way she had never been kissed before. How could she feel nothing but loathing for somewhere that had made her realise how much she could care for a man she had started off by disliking?

Marguerite stood beside her and the slight trembling of the hand that held hers showed just how excited her grandmother was to be going home. René stood the other side of Rowan, and James and Paul Ordin were just a fraction lower down the beach and a little apart, with the solitary mound of Steven's grave beyond them but somehow within the same group. More than once Rowan had noticed the two men glance across there and she could guess how they must be feeling, leaving their old friend behind.

Only an hour ago she had slipped out and broken off a small branch of blossom from one of the orange trees, and brought it down to lay as a last tribute. James had noticed the light pale blossom, already wilting in the sun, the moment they came down there, and he had sent her a faint slow smile of thanks, while Paul had crossed himself and brushed a hand across his eyes.

So far no one had noticed that she had four tiny oranges clasped to her breast and hidden by the arm that held them there; the same oranges that had helped them survive. She had noticed them lying on the table just before they left, and snatched them up at the last minute without anyone noticing.

But René noticed them when he took his eyes for just a moment from the approaching longboat, and he looked at her curiously. 'What on earth have you brought those things for?' he asked. 'Haven't you seen enough of oranges to last you a lifetime, *chérie*?'

He spoke quite loudly enough for James to hear and something in the sharp, almost accusing tone of his voice aroused a lurking suspicion in those ice-blue eyes. He said nothing for the moment, but Rowan felt that he was listening, and curious to know what was making René sound so aggressively sharp at a moment like this.

'Throw them away, darling!' René insisted, and reached as if to take them from her, but Rowan held on to the oranges as tightly as if they were precious gems.

'*No*, René!' James' head turned swiftly and she clung to his enquiring gaze appealingly. 'I—I want to take them with me!'

'Something wrong?' James asked, and Marguerite shook her head.

'Nothing wrong, *mon cher*,' she told him. 'Rowan wants to take the rest of the oranges that you brought us this morning, that's all.' She spoke softly and there was a smile in her eyes that betrayed just how much she knew about the way things stood. 'You want a souvenir, of course, child,' she suggested. 'And James got those for us this morning; it's natural enough.'

'Who needs a souvenir of this place?' René demanded, only too well aware of the implication. 'I'm alive, that's all I care about!'

Marguerite smiled gently and her hand squeezed Rowan's. 'You could say that that too is a souvenir of James, if you think about it, *mon cher* René,' she reminded him gently, and René flushed and hunched his shoulders.

He said nothing more, but Rowan could sense just how tense he was as he stood beside her and stared at the boat that was coming to take them off. There were five men aboard, four at the oars and one who was evidently the captain, judging by his uniform, and the bow had barely time to slip ashore before the five waiting went racing down to meet the boat and the first strangers they had seen for a long time.

Even René managed a quite commendable sprint, in spite of his slight limp, and it was a concerted effort that pulled the boat high, everyone too excited in the first instance to say a word, while the little Venezuelan captain beamed at them all in turn.

'You are from the *Belle o' Dunoon*, yes?' he asked, and James proffered a large hand in welcome.

'James Fraser, captain,' he said, 'and you don't know how thankful we are to see you!'

Formality seemed to be the order of the day, but all the time introductions were being made, the captain's eyes strayed again and again in the direction of the mound higher up the beach. He too crossed himself and murmured an *Ave*, then looked at James with grave dark eyes.

'You did not all survive, Mr Fraser?' he said. 'I am sorry, I had hoped to return your entire complement unscathed.'

'We lost two the first night,' James told him, 'but we only managed to recover one.'

He sounded quite cool about it, but Rowan suspected that the little captain was not so easily deceived, for he placed a hand briefly on his arm and his dark eyes were solemn and sympathetic. 'It is God's will, *señor*, and we must be thankful that so many were saved.'

'We were lucky to find a hut of sorts,' James told him. 'Somebody had been there before us.'

'Ah *sí*.' Again the captain made the appropriate gestures due to the departed. 'There was an American here for some time, but he became sick and his radio was broken, so that he was less fortunate than you, *señor*. He was already dead when his people came to check on him.'

Rowan shuddered, remembering her own uneasy imaginings during the dark hours among the never-silent jungle. But Marguerite was being assisted very gallantly into the longboat by the captain himself and there was no time to muse of things past. René, almost anxiously eager to get aboard, went next, too impatient to wait for assistance and only a little clumsy.

Then James turned and lifted Rowan into his arms, his face close to hers as she put her arm around his neck automatically, smiling into her eyes. 'You'll soon be home now, girl,' he murmured.

Rowan glanced back at the steamy and hostile little island with its glowering jungle and countless watching eyes, and she did not understand why it should suddenly seem so much less awful than it had when she had been forced to exist on its grudging hospitality. There was a misty look in her grey eyes when James set her down gently in the boat and as she slid her arm from around his neck she looked up into his face. Her mouth trembled unsteadily and she longed for the haven of that broad comforting shoulder again.

'I shall miss it,' she confessed in a husky whisper, and for his ears alone.

No one else would even begin to understand, she thought, but James might. Just briefly she felt the light warm touch of his lips on her forehead and caught a faint sound of an exasperated sigh. 'Did I not say you were a daft wee creature?' he demanded, keeping his voice low. 'You'll probably take a quite different view of a lot of things when you get back home again.'

Because she knew exactly what he referred to, Rowan shook her head firmly, and as she watched him swing his long legs over the side of the boat and then slide down beside her, she pursed her lip reproachfully. 'I won't!' she vowed, and knew she meant it.

CHAPTER NINE

THE past four weeks had been the most hectic Rowan ever remembered, and she was thankful that the ballyhoo was all over and things were beginning to return to normal. Not that it hadn't been exciting being in the public eye and being interviewed by press and television reporters, but she was anxious for the whole thing to settle down so that she could give her time to consider more important matters.

René had revelled in it all, and only that morning Rowan had heard from him that he had been commissioned to write a serialised version of his adventures on a tropical island for one of the big Paris dailies. He was wild with excitement, he told her, and promised that she would figure prominently in his story.

It was the latter fact that was causing Rowan so much

unrest, for knowing René's penchant for jumping to conclusions where her feeling for him was concerned, she did
not want it proclaimed to the world that there was a wedding in the offing. Although she had not seen James in
person since their rescue, she felt no differently about him,
and at times longed for him in a way that she would have
ridiculed only a few short months before.

Their rescue ship had brought them to Marseilles, only a
short distance along the coast from Cassis, where the de
Clare vineyards flourished, but James had flown home from
there and there had been no time to talk privately, even
for a few minutes. Once only, when a brief link with Scottish television had been incorporated into an interview
with her and Grand'mère, had they come close to being in
touch, and then the situation had been too bewildering to
make proper communication possible.

Each day she fretted anew because there was no sign
that he even remembered her existence, and each day she
resisted the need she felt to write and tell him that she felt
no differently now that she was home. Because she recalled that he was no stranger to affairs of the heart, she
suspected he looked upon that advice to see how she felt
when she got home, as a kindly way of letting her down—
a way of letting her know that it had been nothing more to
him than a way of keeping them both sane when things
looked bad.

Marguerite had become her normal smart and sophisticated self almost from the moment she set foot in France
again, and a visit to the beauty parlour was all she had
needed to restore her somewhat tarnished image to its
customary glamour. She had enjoyed the interviews and
the television appearances, and might have been at home
in her own *salon* instead of in a television studio.

It was something about the way she smiled as she came
into the room that made Rowan look at her enquiringly
and heave an inward sigh of resignation. Unless she was

very much mistaken, her grandmother had yet another celebratory event lined up, and she might as well learn what it was right away.

'You look very pleased with yourself,' she suggested, with the rather absent little smile that was in evidence all too often lately, and Marguerite's dark eyes slanted her an oblique glance.

'You look much too down in the mouth for a girl who's just been rescued, *chérie*,' she told her. 'You need something to take you out of yourself, and I know just the thing you need.'

Rowan smiled and shook her head, her suspicion confirmed. 'Not another party, Grand'mère, I've been to two this week already, and I'm really not in the mood.'

'You're moping,' Marguerite declared, 'and you need to snap out of it.'

It sounded such a heartless remark coming from her grandmother, and Rowan wondered if she had been too mopingly and obviously unhappy since they came back. Particularly since things had quieted down a bit and she was missing James more than ever. She didn't intend her lip to quiver as it did, but she couldn't think about James without feeling as if she wanted to burst into tears and bury her face into that broad, comforting shoulder again.

'I'm all right, Grand'mère, really,' she insisted, knowing she was not going to be believed, and inevitably Marguerite disagreed.

'You're unhappy,' Marguerite insisted firmly. 'But you'll put on that pretty pale blue dress we bought last week and meet me at Maître Jean's at eight. I have to see Madame Jubert at seven,' she hurried on when she saw an argument looming, 'but I shouldn't be more than an hour.' She came across to her and took Rowan's small wistful face between her hands, smiling down at her for a moment. 'Somehow we have to make you smile again, *petite*, eh?'

Rowan attempted a smile, shaking her head when the

slim beringed hands stroked her cheeks before letting her
go. 'I'm really not——'

'Eight o'clock,' Marguerite interrupted firmly. 'I will
not take no for an answer, *chérie*, and trust me to know
what is good for you, eh?'

There was nothing else to do but shrug resignedly, and
Rowan did appreciate the affection that prompted the suggestion. A quiet dinner for two with her grandmother at
their favourite restaurant might do something to ease
the restless unhappiness she felt at James' absence, and it
might be possible to confide to her grandmother how she
was feeling.

'I'll go,' she promised, smiling. 'I'll put on the blue
dress and see you at eight at Maître Jean's.'

'That's my good girl,' Marguerite approved, and kissed
her forehead. 'I promise you'll feel better for an evening
out, *chérie*!'

It wasn't quite eight o'clock when Rowan arrived, but
Maître Jean himself welcomed her, hovering round and
smilingly leading the way across the crowded restaurant.
'Such an honour to have you with us again, Mademoiselle
de Clare,' he told her, and bobbed his head as he made his
way past the tables at the far end of the room and on towards the open glass doors.

Rowan knew they led on to a paved terrace that had
several small tables set amid the more romantic surroundings of the moonlit gardens, but she could not imagine that
her grandmother had asked to have her meal in the open
air. 'You're quite sure this is the right table?' Rowan ventured, and the man inclined his head confidently.

'Certain, *mademoiselle*!' He saw her seated, then stood
smiling at her, obviously well pleased to have a current
celebrity among his clientele. 'Your meal will be some time
in preparing, Mademoiselle de Clare, if you would care
to stroll in the gardens——'

Rowan nodded, although she had the strangest feeling suddenly; a feeling she could not quite explain or understand. 'When my grandmother arrives——' she began, but that smooth practised bow cut her short as well as an extravagantly casual hand.

'Everything is arranged, *mademoiselle*, please don't concern yourself!'

Rowan watched him go. Something about his manner and the rolling, meaningful motion of his eyes was oddly disconcerting, but she had never known Maître Jean put a foot wrong in the management of his restaurant, so she saw no reason to suppose everything was not, as he said, perfectly well arranged. Perhaps her grandmother had become addicted to the open air since their stay on the island.

Shrugging off the lingering sense of suspicion she felt, she sat at the table for a moment or two, looking out at the thick shrubs and orderly flower-beds that were laid out beyond the steps of the paved terrace. She could go for a stroll while the meal was being prepared, and if her grandmother came while she was gone, Maître Jean would reassure her.

She got to her feet, automatically brushing down the long full skirt of her dress, and revelling in the feel of evening dress again after so long. It would be a long time before she grew blasé about pretty clothes. She glanced up as she went down the steps and the next moment caught her breath audibly, standing stock still on the step and staring ahead into the moonlit garden.

It had been visible for only a second, but the tawny leonine head, silvered by the moon, had been so heart-stoppingly familiar that without her having any idea it was happening, tears sprang into her eyes and trembled there on long dark lashes. 'James!' She whispered it, even though she had meant to call it out, and she was certain suddenly that she knew what it was that Maître Jean had looked so secretive about.

Below the steps was a lawn, before the shrubbery began, and Rowan hurried across it, her steps light and seeming barely to touch the ground. Her heart was thudding so hard that she couldn't hear anything else, but she caught the sudden sound of her name from the narrow path between two rows of shrubs, and twisted quickly in the direction of it.

He was standing under a tree and the moonlight dappled his features with tiny dark shadows, but nothing could have disguised him so well that Rowan wouldn't have known him. Even the unfamiliarity of a dark suit and a shirt and tie that only lightly laid a veneer of civilisation on that primitively earthy body did not deter her.

From the depth of the shadows she caught the gleam of white teeth and when he opened his arms wide she ran into them, hugging so close that she could feel the hard, passionate beat of his heart against her breast. Slowly, lovingly they explored one another's nearness, and James' mouth lightly kissed her eyes, cheeks and neck; moved down to the soft warmth of her throat and neck, then to the shadowy, pale swell below the plunging neck of her dress.

'James, James.' She whispered his name over and over, as if she had to convince herself he was really there, then she lifted her face and looked up into those well-remembered ice-blue eyes. 'James, you—you came for me!'

'I came because I couldn't stay away from you any longer, my sweetheart!' His voice had an unfamiliar huskiness and it shivered through her body like little trickles of ice, as he took stock of her, boldly and uninhibitedly. 'I love you, my own darling, and I think you love me.'

'You know I do!' Rowan told him with only a hint of reproach. 'I've been so unhappy these past four weeks I——'

'Maggie told me!'

Rowan remembered then that it had been her grandmother who set all this up, and she smiled as she shook her head. 'Grand'mère,' she said. 'I should have known!'

'I told her you'd never fall for the idea of her dining tête-à-tête with her granddaughter,' James told her. 'I still can't believe you did.'

Rowan buried her face against him as she had so often done before, and her voice was muffled but utterly content. 'I've been so unhappy I didn't bother to question anything,' she murmured, and James put a big hand to the nape of her neck and tipped back her head.

'Rowan.' He said it softly and with that rolling r that had always intrigued her so. Then he bent and touched her mouth with his, seeking a response from her parted lips that she gave willingly, pressing his own hard down until the softness of her body yielded to the hard steely pressure of his arms, and his kiss was like nothing she had ever known before. His lips moved to the pale vulnerable warmth of her neck and he spoke close to the scented skin, nuzzling aside her silky dark hair. 'I had to be sure, my darling,' he whispered. 'I had to be sure you weren't just —grateful to me!'

'I'm that too,' Rowan murmured against his ear, and brushed her lips to the sun-tanned neck above an unfamiliarly formal collar. 'I owe you my life, Jamie.' She caught her breath, biting her lower lip as she raised her head for a moment and looked up at him. 'I'm sorry,' she whispered. 'You don't like it, but I just——'

James bent and kissed her mouth again, long and lingeringly. 'If you're going to be family,' he said in that intriguingly rolling tone, 'I suppose I'll have to allow you to slip up occasionally.' His eyes smiled down at her, warm with that familiar and secret look that René had so disliked. 'You *are* going to marry me, aren't you?' he asked, but his look suggested that he had no doubt at all what her answer would be.

'I love you,' Rowan whispered, and he stroked his big

hand through her hair, gentle as he always was.

'I don't know what I'd have done if you *had* decided you didn't after all,' he confessed.

Rowan looked down at the smart grey tie he wore and traced its pattern with the tip of a finger while she spoke. 'Shall—I mean, will we be announcing it soon?' she asked, and he regarded her with his head to one side and a faintly quizzical smile.

'As soon as you like, my darling. Why?'

She heaved a deep sigh, then snuggled up close to him again, as she had so often done when things were beyond her. 'René's writing about his experiences in one of the big dailies,' she said, 'and he's promised that I shall figure prominently in his story. I—I wouldn't like him to look foolish because he took things for granted.'

'Poor old René,' he said, and brushed the hair from her brow with his lips. 'Don't worry, my love, I'll let him know how things stand before he tells the world that you're *his* girl.'

'Gently,' Rowan pleaded, and James kissed her mouth.

'Of course,' he agreed. 'Aren't I always?'

'Yes, of course.' But when next he kissed her, Rowan wondered if perhaps he wasn't always, although she found no cause for complaint.

Mills & Boon Classics

The very best of Mills & Boon
romances, brought back for those of you
who missed reading them when they
were first published.

In
July
we bring back the following four
great romantic titles.

SONG IN MY HEART
by Rachel Lindsay

When Sara's brother got into serious trouble, she first gave up
her training as an opera singer to help him and then persuaded
his employer in the Combined Television Company to give
him another chance. Her unselfishness had its reward — for it
led her to a new, glittering career, and at last to the love of
her life.

THE GLASS CASTLE
by Violet Winspear

'Out in the East they say that the mind of a woman is a
jungle, and it is the one jungle in which a man should never get
lost.' That was the code by which the arrogant Edwin Trequair
lived — or so he told Heron. Why then did he ask her to marry
him?

INTERLUDE IN ARCADY
by Margery Hilton

When Nicola agreed to accompany Marcus Hillary to his hide-
out on the Yorkshire moors, she had no illusions. Marcus was
only using her as a means of warding off certain predatory
females while he finished writing his new play. So, when they
began to descend on Arcady, why should she find herself
beginning to mind?

THE INNOCENT INVADER
by Anne Mather

Sarah, straight from a convent, went out wide-eyed with
excitement to the West Indies to a job as governess to the
small wards of Jason de Cordova. And had the bad luck to fall
in love with her employer — who was not only married but
had every intention of staying married! How could she cope
with the heartbreak?

If you have difficulty in obtaining any of these books through
your local paperback retailer, write to:
Mills & Boon Reader Service
P.O. Box 236, Thornton Road, Croydon, Surrey, CR9 3RU.

The Mills & Boon Rose is the Rose of Romance

Every month there are ten new titles to choose from — ten new stories about people falling in love, people you want to read about, people in exciting, far-away places. Choose Mills & Boon. It's your way of relaxing.

July's titles are:

CHANCE MEETING by *Kay Thorpe*
Lee Brent was socially and financially right out of Sharon's league, and the last thing she wanted was to discover why he had really married her . . .

PRISONER IN PARADISE by *Marjorie Lewty*
Stranded in Mexico, Sara's rescuer was the formidable Jason Knight, who made no secret of his low opinion of her.

SET THE STARS ON FIRE by *Sally Wentworth*
When actress Lori West joined a film company in Rhodes, she was aware of hostility from everyone there — in particular from the director, Lewis Brent.

HALF A WORLD AWAY by *Gloria Bevan*
On a trip to New Zealand, Nicola met and fell in love with Keith Lorimer, but he didn't seem to feel anything but friendship for her . . .

YESTERDAY'S SCARS by *Carole Mortimer*
Because of what had once passed between Hazel and her stern cousin-guardian Rafe Savage, she found he was now bitter and unforgiving, scarred in more than body . . .

CAROLINE'S WATERLOO by *Betty Neels*
Could Caroline settle for a marriage to the imposing Professor Radinck Thoe van Erckelens when it was clear that there was to be no romance involved?

THE LEO MAN by *Rebecca Stratton*
James Fraser was a typical Leo man, thought Rowan — bossy! But she found herself rapidly revising her opinion.

A RING FOR A FORTUNE by *Lilian Peake*
Sloan Lancaster agreed to marry Jasmine so that she could inherit her grandfather's fortune, although Sloan made no pretence of feeling anything for her but contempt . . .

MISS HIGH AND MIGHTY by *Margaret Rome*
How could Jade convince her husband, the lordly Dom Diego da Luz Pereira da Silves, that he was wrong to accuse her of marrying him for his money?

THE BUTTERFLY AND THE BARON by *Margaret Way*
Renee Dalton was a rich society butterfly, and the forceful, down-to-earth Nick Garbutt had no opinion of her at all.

Doctor Nurse Romances

and July's
stories of romantic relationships behind the scenes
of modern medical life are:

OMEN FOR LOVE
by Esther Boyd

When Nurse Carol Baxter decided that she was tired of
taking orders from her stuffy fiancé, she left him to
join Dr Ian Morrison's immunisation programme in the
jungles of Peru — and found herself at the beck and call
of another dictator! Was it only a coincidence that
the flower Ian gave her was regarded as a bad omen in
Peru?

JET NURSE
by Muriel Janes

When Sheelagh's perfect future with Doctor Michael
Kelman did not materialise, she took to the skies as a
jet nurse — and found a glamorous pilot, Terry
Fitzsimmons, who was only too willing to take Michael's
place. But were Sheelagh's feet too firmly on the ground
for her to forget Michael — and *real* nursing — so easily?